THE WISHING SEED

NOVELS BY ALISSA J. ZAVALIANOS

The Earth-Treader

THE WISHING SEED

ALISSA J. ZAVALIANOS

Printed in the United States of America

Cover design by Germancreative
Interior Formatting by Michelle M. Bruhn
Edited by Jordan Yaworski

ISBN 978-1-7361371-4-7 (paperback)
ISBN 978-1-7361371-3-0 (hardcover)
ISBN 978-1-7361371-5-4 (ebook)

*To all the children who feel the pressure
of growing up, of fitting in,
and of finding your own voice...
You're not alone and you never will be.*

*"Likewise, every good tree bears good fruit,
but a bad tree bears bad fruit."*
Matthew 7:17

*"Someday you will be old enough to
start reading fairy tales again."*
C.S. Lewis

Table of Contents

Chapter 1

The Seed

It was a cool summer day, the kind that often shows the telltale signs of the approach of autumn. Though the new season was still a few weeks away, tomorrow was Mona's first day of seventh grade. And if entering another year of middle school wasn't already frightening enough, she was attending a new school. Which meant new friends, new teachers, new classes, new school lunches…To sum it up nicely, it was a whole lot of change and she had a whole lot of nerves.

It wasn't that she hated school. In fact, she quite enjoyed learning. But ever since her father had switched jobs and moved their family of four to a small town in New Hampshire, things had never felt the same. Mona had only known Arizona and its dry weather, the beautiful red rocks of Sedona, and the slow-paced culture. Having to abandon what she called home to travel to New England was like stepping onto a different planet. Not to mention a different time zone.

Her younger sister Lisa didn't seem all that bothered, though. She was entering the fifth grade, and that year was usually awkward enough as it were with straddling the line between elementary and middle school. New kids entered fifth grade every year, and it would always be an awkward time for everyone no matter what school one went to. Whereas by seventh grade, most people had their already established friend groups.

Mona tightened the blanket around her shoulders, the tall blades of grass tickling her toes. Despite the cooler weather, she always liked being barefoot.

She'd been in this new home for a few weeks, and having already experienced a good dose of New England humidity, she was thankful today hadn't provoked her curly hair into a giant ball of frizz. Small victories.

Mona was staring at the border of trees lining the edge of the woods, their small, but comfortable, cottage house behind her. Of all the things not to like about the move, the new house hadn't been one of them. Nor the woods. She actually liked her cozy, angular room with a window seat, and she liked it even more that it provided an excellent view of their backyard.

The front yard was a decent size too with a long, winding driveway, and the house was set back enough to retain some privacy though the main road was close by.

Mona continued to stare at the tall conifers and pines and decided to get up and explore. One could only sit still for so long anyways, and seeing as tomorrow would be the start of sitting still for the foreseeable future, she silently berated herself for having sat at all.

As she walked toward the trees, she felt that something was beckoning her closer, like an invisible string was tugging somewhere in the back of her mind or like a thought that was impossible to let go of. She couldn't explain it, it was just something she felt to be true.

Mona stopped once her feet hit the tree line. She tilted her head back and inwardly gasped. When she glanced at the sky, she thought she saw an oddly shaped cloud. It resembled a pirate ship—strikingly so. It was intricately detailed and seemed to shimmer with a sheen of silver.

She rubbed her eyes and looked once more, but it had vanished. *How odd.* It must have been a trick of the light or a particle in the wind. Still, she couldn't shake the feeling that perhaps it meant something more.

The idea excited her. She'd always been a dreamer with a wild imagination. But growing up had begun to snuff some of that out, replacing her musings with practicality. Still, she fought against the expectation that growing up meant she needed to surrender her imagination.

Even now, Mona wanted to continue dreaming, but all that was left were the looming trees towering before her; they sliced through the sky like knives through a loaf of bread.

If only she could climb way up high and pretend she was a squirrel, then perhaps she could escape going to school. She'd heard plenty of stories growing up, and though turning into a squirrel might be next to impossible, she'd read enough about transportable wardrobes, magic beanstalks, or tall trees like the ones before her, to know that perhaps other realms could be reached—like Narnia, Hogwarts, or even Neverland. If only she could spend the school hours there instead!

But how to get there? Maybe she should look for a seed and grow her own tree. The magic only worked if one grew the plant themselves. Everyone knew that—at least that's what all the stories said.

Deep down, Mona knew the odds of finding and planting anything magical were next to none, but it gave her something to do. And with only so much time before the start of school, it gave her newfound hope, if only slightly.

Mona stepped into the shade of the conifers, smiling over her clever plan no matter how ridiculous it seemed. If anything, this would be her one last adventure before the dreaded school year, so she wanted to make it count.

Maybe she'd even make it home before supper.

* * *

Dinner that night was unbearable, let alone trying to keep anything down. Mona fidgeted in her seat like a fish on land, her hands resting atop her lap underneath the table.

"My goodness, Mona, ants in your pants much?" Her father chuckled as he set his newspaper on the kitchen table and took another bite of steak. He, along with her mother and sister, were all eyeing Mona closely with looks of bemused fascination.

"Honey, there's nothing to be afraid of tomorrow. I'm sure you will make plenty of new friends," her mom said warmly.

"It looks like she has to go to the bathroom," Lisa blurted as she stuffed a cooked tomato in her mouth.

Mona silently thanked her.

"Yes! The bathroom, I forgot to go before dinner. May I please be excused?" Mona felt the lie escape her lips as she left her chair and took the stairs two at a time. She remembered to lock the bathroom door behind her, but only just, before reaching inside her pocket.

In her palm rested the oddest-looking seed she'd ever seen: it was hairy with brown roots coming off in all directions, but it continued to shimmer a metallic silver when the light hit it just right.

That's what had drawn her attention to the seed in the first place. But that wasn't all she'd found.

On her recent quest in the woods, she'd also discovered a secret hideout in her backyard—a clearing that was hard to discern from any angle—and in stepping into it, the world opened up to her in a small, conical grove of fall colors on every side. There wasn't much in the midst of the enclosure save for a few faerie houses on the outskirts and a shimmering seed at its center, beckoning her closer with its beauty. Mona had tentatively walked toward the seed and picked it up only to be compelled to look skyward. There in the clouds, the same ship from earlier had been hovering above the tree line, as if waiting. But in a wink, it had vanished once again.

As Mona turned the seed over in her hand, the bathroom lights paling in comparison to its silver luster, she couldn't help but think about the significance of the strange, silver cloud. Had it been a *real* ship, she would have thought this seed came from it.

But it couldn't be real. Just like Mona knew deep down

that the chances of growing a beanstalk or other and finding a magical realm were rather slim. It was only her faith that was keeping her going. She had to at least try.

Mona was hopeful that this seed would be the ticket to her freedom. All she had to do was wait until her parents went to bed and then plant it in the moonlight. For a magic seed would only sprout when planted at the onset of the moon. Everyone knew that. And then she would climb up its leafy stalk the following morning, and no one would be the wiser. That was her childlike hope at least.

Fighting the temptation to linger, Mona quickly stuck the seed in the cabinet above the sink, high enough that Lisa wouldn't see it and close enough for Mona to still reach. But it wouldn't be there for long. She only had to wait a few more hours, and then, it would be time to plant!

* * *

Mona lay in bed, counting the seconds as they ticked by on her clock.

"Nine, ten, eleven, twelve…" She heard a door click shut at the far end of the hall. If she were correct, that now meant everyone was in bed.

"Thirteen, fourteen, fifteen, sixteen…" Mona craned her

neck against her pillow to see if she detected any other sounds. All was silent, but it was best to wait a few more seconds.

"Seventeen, eighteen, nineteen, twenty…" Still no noise.

Mona carefully crawled out of bed, threw on her bathrobe, and made for the bathroom. There, she quietly locked the door behind her and flicked on the light switch. The bright bulb made her eyes scream before they adjusted to her surroundings. She opened the cabinet above the sink and felt for the hairy seed. Relief flooded through her body when her fingers felt its familiar form, clutching it tightly before bringing it to her chest. She glanced at it once more before sticking it in her pocket.

Now onto the window.

This was the only window in the house without a screen, and seeing as there was a hearty oak with its branches conveniently close to the house, it would be foolish not to go this way. Plus, it was an easy route to the backyard without having to make much noise. The stairs to downstairs creaked on all their planks and any door on the main floor squeaked upon opening. Mona didn't want to risk waking anyone. The bathroom was the safest, and quietest, bet.

Mona unlocked the window and placed two hands on the glass frame, pushing upward. It gave a slight squeak as old paint grated against the wood, but it wasn't too loud to be heard beyond the bathroom. She stepped on the toilet seat and climbed onto the window's ledge. Being long and limber had its advantages, but currently squeezing through the small frame was proving difficult. At least it would help her reach the tree more easily.

Mona silently counted to three before propelling herself off the ledge and landing gently on the thick branch nearest the house. Her momentum carried her towards its trunk as she gingerly made her way down and onto the cool ground.

She'd forgotten to put on shoes, but the feeling of the dewy grass felt promising. There would be enough moisture in the earth tonight to water the seed.

Quickly so as not to be gone too long, Mona proceeded to the secret location she'd found earlier—the grove tucked away in the woods. It seemed like the perfect place to plant her seed since that's where she'd found it.

Her steps were slow and careful, despite the adrenaline coursing through her body; if she walked any faster, she was sure a loose twig or briar would get lodged in her foot.

When she finally reached the hidden spot, the moonlight poured into the circular grove and illuminated the ground and surrounding faerie houses with a gentle halo of silver. A shiver ran down her spine and the back of her neck pricked with gooseflesh. If Mona didn't know any better, the enclosure almost seemed to be watching her—was this some sort of magic?

Mona stepped closer and gulped. She'd push aside her fears; the faster she planted the seed, the faster she could get back to bed. Her parents would know something was up if she remained "locked" in the bathroom all night. But how to dig a hole?

Mona looked around and her gaze alighted once more upon the faerie houses. They were of varying sizes and shapes, some made out of logs and twigs, a few from mushrooms and pinecones, and others constructed with various gardening tools. She eyed a shovel currently being used as a roof for one of the homes and quickly snatched it to begin digging.

Someone had been here before to construct the houses, and Mona guessed it must have been the last homeowners. But something nagged at the back of her mind, telling her that she was wrong. There were so many and they were all so intricate and weathered, that she couldn't help but feel that they had been here for ages.

Even the grove itself had felt untouched upon her first arrival, like a forgotten memory, as if no one had stepped foot in it for a long time. How was that possible?

Within a few minutes, Mona had created a big enough hole for the seed. Reaching into her pocket, she withdrew her precious talisman and held it in her hands.

"Please grow, please," she whispered into it. "I don't want to go to school. I wish…I wish for a way to escape it all." And for added measure, "Please, God. I don't want anything to change." She kissed the seed before placing it into the hole, her prayers along with it. A beanstalk might not grow, but at least she knew God was listening.

As quickly as the hole was dug, it was just as quickly covered back up. Mona gave the faerie house back its roof and brushed the dirt from her hands.

She looked once more at the ground and gasped. Sure enough, moonlight now streamed from the sky in a concentrated silvery beam, alighting upon the exact spot where she'd just planted the seed.

Mona bit her lip in anticipation but knew she shouldn't linger. She had to get back to the bathroom!

Careful once more not to lodge something sharp in her feet, Mona picked her way through the short span of woods and ran back to the tree beside her house. Instantly, she began to climb, her long limbs matching those of the tree's. At the top, she climbed back through the open window, finding it even more difficult to get inside than it was to get out.

Once inside, she quickly relocked the window and washed her hands. But before leaving, she flushed the toilet for good measure. If anyone was awake, she'd rather let them believe she'd been in the bathroom so long because dinner hadn't sat well in her stomach. The small act made her feel better.

As Mona walked quietly back to her room and settled into bed, she only hoped her plan had worked. The morning couldn't come soon enough.

Chapter 2

Resisting the Change

"Mona!" a voice called out to her. But it was too early, surely there was more time.

"Mona Ramone!" The voice came again, but now more frantic. "Wake up! You don't want to ignore me, especially on your first day of school!" The voice of her homeroom teacher finally registered, and as Mona's heart sped up from embarrassment, she opened her eyes to see a very angry woman looming over her. But it wasn't her teacher, it was just her mother.

Mona breathed a quick sigh of relief. It had only been a dream, a nightmare rather. She wasn't *actually* in school.

"It's nearly 6:30 and you're supposed to be at school in half an hour! Why didn't you get up at six like I asked you to?" Her mother was over by her curtains, thrusting them open and letting the morning light pour into the room. "You still need to shower and get dressed and eat a decent breakfast! I can't send you to school with an empty stomach!" She walked over to the closet and reached toward the back, yanking out Mona's least favorite dress: a coral-colored, knee-length abomination that clung awkwardly to all the wrong places. "This is just darling, Mona! Why don't you wear this today?"

Mona was still blinking her eyes from having overslept, the idea of putting that horrible dress on seeming more of a nightmare than falling asleep in class. Perhaps she *had* stayed up too late last night.

"Up, up! You don't have much time!" Exasperated, her mother quickly left Mona's room and made her way downstairs, the sound of the blender signifying the onset of breakfast.

Mona didn't want to get up, the thought of staying in bed sounding more appealing even if it meant being late on her first day of school. But then she remembered—the seed! Stifling the urge to run outside in her pajamas, Mona shot out of bed, showering and dressing with lightning speed in the process. She didn't want to go to school, but she hoped that by at least taking the time to look presentable, it would help to mollify her mother.

After getting ready in under ten minutes, choosing instead to wear light-wash denim jeans with a knotted T-shirt featuring Cathedral Rock in Sedona, Mona made her way downstairs. She bypassed the noisy kitchen, her frantic mother, and hungry Lisa to visit the backyard and the skepticism of new growth. Throwing on her sneakers, she exited the house with her mother's protestations echoing in the background.

"What about breakfast?" she yelled.

But Mona kept walking. She'd have plenty of time to eat after she checked on the supposed beanstalk.

If the *magic* had worked, she'd be climbing its thick, leafy vines and escaping into another world where her new school wouldn't be able to find her. But she had little faith that the seed had actually sprouted. Did she even believe in magic in the first place?

Mona stumbled into the clearing, gooseflesh pricking the nape of her neck as she surveyed the spectacle before her. Complete awe and bitter disappointment warred inside her chest, uncertain which of the two would win. *Apparently, magic does exist!*

Mona *had* planted some sort of magical seed, for there was now a full-grown tree in its place. But that was all. No giant, leafy vines had climbed into the sky—no covering of clouds above to indicate a hidden world at the top. It was, in fact, a very boring tree, shorter than the pines and firs encircling it and none too wide, either. It was positively abysmal, and Mona wondered what good was magic if it only produced less than average trees.

The only things worth noticing were the clusters of orange berries attached to its branches. They resembled apricots and peaches, but they were indeed smaller, like a raspberry or grape. But these bright orange fruits were unlike anything Mona had ever seen and were hardly worth celebrating.

"I don't know what to think," Mona said in the direction of the tree. "You were supposed to help me get out of school! You were supposed to change everything!" Mona scrutinized the timber before her, part of her wanting to marvel at it. The magic *had* worked after all, and the thought made her stomach somersault.

She reached a hand out to touch the fruit, her fingertips tingling upon contact. She found both the texture and aroma rather pleasant. She'd been warned as a child never to eat foreign berries or mushrooms for fear of being poisoned, but this tree wouldn't mean any harm. *Right?*

It *was* magical, but surely the magic wouldn't be poisonous. And if this tree wouldn't provide her the escape she so desperately needed, perhaps the secret lied within the berries themselves.

Mona quickly picked a handful and put them in her pocket before returning to the house.

In the kitchen, her mom grabbed her purse and bags from off the counter and made her way to the garage. "Your backpack and lunch are on the bench by the door, Mona! Make sure to grab them before getting in the car—Lisa, hurry up in the bathroom. We're going!" her mom shouted toward the stairs.

Lisa came down them a few seconds later, her blue backpack strung over her shoulder and her stuffed elephant in her hands.

Mona could tell Lisa was nervous; she always brought Ellie with her to new places, and school was no exception. Mona only hoped no one would make fun of her sister for bringing a stuffed animal to the first day of fifth grade. Instantly, Mona felt compassion replace some of the apprehension in her gut. She wasn't the only one dreading this new school.

"I told you to eat breakfast, Mona! You'll have to eat the extra granola bar I packed in your bag to hold you over until lunch," her mom spoke over her shoulder as the three of them exited the house and into the garage.

The empty spot next to the white minivan indicated that

her father had already left for work. As the Museum of Fine Arts' new curator, he had to leave early every morning to beat the Boston traffic.

"Thanks," Mona said. She grabbed her belongings before taking the passenger's seat.

Lisa climbed into the back and their mom took the driver's.

While the garage door opened and her mom was looking into the mirrors to back out, Mona took the opportunity to fish out the orange fruits from her pocket and place them in the paper bag. She was relieved her mother hadn't seen her, but when she looked at her sister through the reflection in the side mirror, Lisa's eyes quickly darted downward, fixed on the elephant in her hands.

"What a beautiful sunny day!" her mom began as their minivan backed into the street and the garage door closed. As she shifted the car into drive, they were now beginning the short ride to what Mona felt was one step closer to her doom.

Her nerves were as fragile as a petal, tempting to make her fall apart should anything jostle her. She didn't want to talk about the sun. She was still mourning her loss of the hidden world above the trees, of her fleeting glimpse into avoiding the seventh grade. She loathed everything about today: this morning, this car, her dad's new job, and most of all, the fact that she had to go to school. And the seed hadn't seemed to help any of those problems. True, it *hadn't* promised to grow into anything useful in the first place, but still, she had put enough hope in it to feel crushed by its failure.

So much for believing in fairy tales.

The drive ended too soon as their white van pulled up to a large brick building with the words *Pine View Middle School* in big block letters across the top. Surrounding the building, as it was appropriately named, were clusters and clusters of pine trees. Mona noted a playground peeking out from the back with basketball courts, a jungle gym, and picnic tables.

Perhaps if I can just make it to recess, then I can retreat behind the trees. This thought helped to steady Mona's nerves as the butterflies began to dance unruly rhythmic patterns in her stomach.

Her mom pulled into the drop-off lane where she saw other parents sending their kids to the slaughter—at least that's how it felt.

Mona reluctantly opened her door and got out of the car. Lisa followed suit. But before they said goodbye to their mom, she motioned them to the window.

"Now, I know you girls are probably nervous on your first day. And that's completely normal, but today will be a good day. I want you both to believe that. And I can't wait to hear all about it when I pick you up at 2:30." Their mom looked like she was trying to hold back tears. "I know this move has been challenging for you, but I trust it's all for the best. I'm so proud of you, and I love you both very much."

"We love you too, Mom," Mona and Lisa said at the same time, tugging their backpacks tighter around their shoulders, Mona gripping tightly to her lunch bag and Lisa practically suffocating her stuffed elephant.

"I'll be seeing you at 2:30!" their mom repeated before she turned the van in the direction of her work.

All that remained was for Mona and Lisa to make the daunting trek inside and to their homerooms.

"I'm scared, Mone," Lisa sighed deeply as she walked next to her sister. "What if they don't like me?"

"How could they not like a squirt like you? Trust me, Leese, everyone is scared on their first day," Mona assured her.

"Really? How can you know that?" Lisa looked at her with curious eyes. "You're not scared, are you?"

"Because…" Mona didn't want to admit she was nervous herself. "…I just know these things. But there's nothing to fear, we have each other." She gave her sister what felt like a convincing smile, and Lisa, having been satisfied by the answer, appeared to loosen her hold on the elephant's neck. Now if only Mona could believe the words herself.

The two girls crossed the threshold into the building. Once inside, they were instructed on where to go and were given the numbers to their homerooms. Due to the entire school functioning under the middle school format, Lisa was told she would also be following a block schedule like Mona. The sisters glanced at their schedules and realized they had different lunch periods. It also appeared that only fifth and sixth-graders received recess, not seventh and eighth-graders.

Mona sighed. *So much for having each other.* Lunch was one of the most socially awkward times of the day. *And so much for escaping behind the trees.* Mona would be stuck inside all day with the same group of kids who she had a feeling weren't interested in being her friends.

The first bell rang, signifying the five minutes remaining before classes began. Mona quickly hugged Lisa and said she'd find her at dismissal.

Lisa nodded and the two parted ways.

Mona looked at her slip of paper which read 102 C, her homeroom. Walking the hallway to that numbered doorway felt like she was walking into a living nightmare.

Chapter 3

Bitter Fruit

Mona couldn't wait to go home. Already she had gone through first period Language Arts and second period Algebra I, but sitting through third period Geography was unbearable. The school felt a little too clean, and rooms too fluorescent, the atmosphere altogether unpreferable. True, there were at least a couple of different kids in each class, allowing the chance that perhaps one of them would want to be her friend, but she couldn't shake the feeling that she didn't belong. That perhaps her perpetually tanned skin and unruly, curly hair were dead giveaways that she was an imposter to the East Coast.

She was used to the arid climate of the desert; here, there was so much moisture in the air that it was as if her skin was constantly wet. She was sure it didn't look good and added to the reason why no one had talked to her yet.

To make matters worse, in class they were reviewing the geographical regions and climate zones of the United States. Without even having raised her hand, Mona was called on.

"Let's see, ah yes, Ms. Ramone, is it?" her teacher Mr. Frankweiler asked. He was tall and lean with the biggest wire-rimmed spectacles. He wore suspenders and a tweed overcoat like he was stuck somewhere between the mid-1800s to early 1900s. But the worst part was his voluminous mustache that rested like a caterpillar above his upper lip.

"Ye-yes, sir?" Mona stuttered, taken completely by surprise.

"You're new here, if I presume correctly, and from Arizona. The climate there is rather different, don't you think?" he asked, his eyes peering into hers and challenging her to speak.

"Uh, yes, sir." Mona gulped. She hoped she wouldn't have to say anymore. Already too much attention was being drawn in her direction.

"I've never been, but the desert has always fascinated me. Perhaps you'd like to stand in front of the class and tell us about where you lived. You can start us off—Pollie Archibald, you may go next seeing as you're from Michigan,"

Mr. Frankweiler addressed the girl sitting a few desks behind her and then motioned for Mona to step forward.

If only the floor would swallow her whole. It was one thing to go to school and blend into the crowd, but to be forced to stand in front of her class like an exotic bird on display, her differences plastered across her face like a sign outside a store, it was too much. And on the first day too!

Mona didn't want to move, but despite her reluctance, her teacher gestured for her to go to the front of the class.

What was she to say?

"I, uh…um," Mona stuttered.

"Why don't you tell us about where you're from, what your neighborhood was like," Mr. Frankweiler prodded, his mustache fluttering with each exhaustion of his breath.

Mona couldn't stop looking at it. She'd prefer being dared to shave it off than to stand before the class, speaking to them about what she missed more than anything in the world.

"It, it was really warm…" Mona began. She looked at her classmates, some of them yawning and others who seemed to roll their eyes. They found her boring!

Her nerves seeking to take full control, Mona swallowed the lump in her throat and stilled her fidgeting hands by gripping them tightly into fists by her sides. She needed to get this over with…

"Sedona is red. The world I lived in was red, and here it's very brown and green. The trees in the desert are different, and we have lots of snakes and scorpions compared to here…"

The minutes ticked by slowly as she spoke, the room spinning before her eyes. Her vision blurred, her palms grew unusually clammy in their fists, and her tongue felt two times too big. *Will this torture never end?*

Finally, it seemed Mr. Frankweiler had had enough and gestured for Pollie to go next.

It's about time. When Mona finally sat and Pollie took the floor, followed by a Thomas from California and a José from Texas, only then did her heartbeat begin to settle. Apparently, she wasn't the only "new" student after all—there were many from all over the country.

The thought was somewhat comforting, but it was still a shock to get up and speak on the first day of seventh grade. It had felt like a blur, an impossible task, but she had done it, and she silently wished she'd never have to do something like that again.

The bell finally rang, signaling it was time for lunch. Mona felt herself grow anxious once more. The social hour. This was even more telling than class time. This was the truest test and indicator of just how dull someone appeared. Mona had no friends; she was dull already.

She made her way into the lunchroom and found a vacant table in the back corner near a large window. She quickly sat down and tried to tune out the loudness of the cafeteria.

Mona opened her paper bag and while taking out her sandwich, small orange fruits spilled onto the table and the floor. She'd forgotten about the berries!

Quickly so as not to draw more attention, Mona picked up the remaining fruits from the table and shoved them into her bag. The ones on the floor she kicked and sent them careening who-knew-where.

She chanced a glance to see if anyone had noticed, but no one was looking. As she peered into the bag, she saw the bright orange of the berries staring back at her, their color and aroma beckoning her to taste. Perhaps she should. Maybe it would be the magic she had sought earlier, the answer to getting out of school. If she were lucky, perhaps she would disappear.

Mona didn't think; instead, she popped one berry into her mouth. When the flavor hit her tongue, she found it unusually bitter—definitely not pleasant. She swallowed with difficulty and was beginning to feel her heart race even more than before, her anxious pulse unsettling. *Odd.*

Perhaps if she just ate one more…she took another bite and spat the second fruit into a napkin, wiping the juice from her lips. The second berry tasted even worse, filling her with greater apprehension than before.

"What's wrong with these?" Mona stared at the remaining berries, her patience growing thin. "So much for wishing on that tree. So much for trying to avoid school!"

"Who are you talking to?"

A voice broke through her reveries, causing Mona to jump and almost choke on her words.

It was the new girl Pollie from Geography.

"Uh, hello, um, no one!" Mona stuttered as she turned toward the brown-haired girl, her heart racing from being caught off guard. She hadn't seen Pollie sneak up on her.

"Mind if I sit here?" Pollie questioned, her eyes kind.

"Oh, um, yes!" Mona was surprised that someone would want to sit with her, especially after overhearing her talk to herself. But then Pollie's gaze looked slightly confused, unsure if she should sit. "I mean no, I don't mind."

Pollie smiled and took a seat, her wavy, brown hair swaying behind her. "So, you're from Arizona, huh? Sounds like a neat place." She pulled her sandwich out of her lunch bag and began to eat.

Mona remembered she hadn't eaten hers yet, so she quickly undid the wrapping of her sandwich and began to eat as well. It was turkey and cheese, her favorite.

"Yeah, I miss it." The truth poured out before Mona had a chance to stop it. Admitting that she missed Arizona was like admitting that she hated her new school, admitting that she longed for friendship.

"I thought I'd feel the same way about Michigan, but after moving around so much, you kinda forget what home's really like," Pollie replied, her expression somber as she took another bite of her sandwich.

"You haven't only lived in Michigan?" Mona asked between bites of food.

"I've lived all over! I grew up in London then moved to Iceland for a few months before coming to the U.S. I've lived in Oregon, Colorado, South Dakota, and most recently Michigan before coming here. But not many people know that long history." Pollie shrugged, taking a bite of her sandwich.

London. That explained Pollie's slight accent. Mona had thought Pollie sounded interesting while speaking in class, and now she knew why. "But why move so often?" Mona suddenly felt guilty for her reluctance to move across the country. Pollie's life felt like a living nightmare.

"My mom grows restless easily and needs to keep moving. She's been this way ever since our time in London, but she won't tell me why…"

Mona was growing thirsty as she listened to Pollie talk.

She reached for her juice pouch, realizing the straw was still in the bottom of her lunch bag. She opened it again only to have more orange berries fall onto the table.

"I'm guessing something happened, but I'm not sure what. My dad couldn't stand it though…hey, what are those?" Pollie's gaze was now directed to the strange-looking fruit before them.

Mona's cheeks heated. "They're nothing!" Not wanting Pollie to question further, Mona tried to shove them back into the bag. But the fruit seemed to evade her grasp.

Pollie picked one up and examined it closely. "I've never seen something like this before. It doesn't look real. What are these?" she questioned.

"I, uh…I'm not sure," Mona replied in truth, still in shock that Pollie was holding one of the orange berries between her fingers.

"Mind if I try it?" Pollie asked.

"I, um…I wouldn't if I were you," Mona said, remembering the bitter taste in her mouth. The fruit had tasted awful and with her seemingly new friend, she didn't want to scare Pollie away. Nor did she want Pollie to find out about the *magic*.

"Why not?" Pollie laughed, bringing the orange berry closer to her eyes, peering at it skeptically.

"Just trust me." Mona tried taking the fruit back, but Pollie only held it closer.

"Did you have one?" Pollie questioned.

"I did, and it tasted gross." Mona didn't want her new friend to experience the same thing.

"It can't be that bad! It looks delicious!" Pollie brought the fruit closer to her mouth and before Mona could stop her, she bit into it. A golden juice leaked from the split skin, trickling from her mouth and onto the table. Mona stared in shock, afraid of the growing look on Pollie's face; it was one of utter disgust.

"Bleh…you were right…it's super bitter!" Pollie spat the remaining fruit out and shuddered. "I feel strange all of a sudden, like kinda weirded out. I don't really know." Pollie spoke like she had seen the underside of a rotten floorboard, her face contorting in extreme displeasure.

"I *had* warned you…" Mona's cheeks reddened from embarrassment, her heart dropping for the second time that day. Surely the fruit hadn't been *that* bad, had it? The bitter remnants on her tastebuds were proof that it had. The orange berries were nothing short of awful and their aftertaste was unsettling, to say the least.

Now Mona would lose her only friend because of them.

"Where did you get something this awful? The

supermarket should know about this before they sell more." Pollie picked up her napkin to scrub her tongue before throwing the rest of the fruit away.

Mona contemplated whether or not she should keep it a secret. Perhaps Pollie could be trusted, but this magical tree had only just grown last night. Perhaps if she gave it another day, then the fruit would taste better?

"I don't know, my mom usually does the grocery shopping." Mona lied again. It just occurred to her that by her not wanting to go to school, she had now lied a handful of times—more than she'd ever lied in her entire life. Growing up in the church and going to Sunday school had warned her against it, that lying was a slippery slope…had she learned nothing?

"Well, wherever they're from, it seems they had a run-in with some bad fruit. You know how the saying goes: '*One bad apple ruins the bunch!*' That could have happened to them." Pollie finished her sandwich and took a sip from her water bottle. She didn't show any signs of leaving anytime soon, so perhaps Mona had misjudged her.

Maybe school wouldn't be so bad after all if Pollie decided to stick around and be her friend. Mona hadn't believed it to be possible, but it seemed she *had* made a friend on her first day after all. And that made her feel guilty about the lie she told Pollie about the fruit.

"It's a good thought," Mona replied, not really thinking. As much as Pollie's words made sense, these fruits hadn't been around any other fruits in a store. They came straight from the tree itself. Mona couldn't help but wonder: what did that say about the seed, then?

Chapter 4

Discontent with it All

"Already, Lisa? You were quite the social butterfly on the first day!" Her mother laughed warmly.

The car ride home from school was filled with Lisa's exciting stories about her kind teachers and new friend group at recess. She was telling everyone her plans to invite her friends over so they could see her house. It seemed that Lisa had acclimated to her new environment even better than Mona had anticipated. Ellie was now stuffed deeply inside Lisa's backpack, practically forgotten. Just more proof that the day had gone better than expected.

Despite it being their first day, Lisa was averaging about five new friends whereas Mona had only one. Still, at least she had one.

Mona recounted her day to eager ears but felt her words fall flat, her mind drifting back to the fruit. She hadn't mentioned them to anyone, save for Pollie, but even then, she hadn't told the whole truth. This was still her secret. And right when she got home, she was going to visit the tree. Maybe it would reveal *its* secrets.

The car pulled into the garage and the girls were out of the car before their mother even had the chance to open her door. Mona rushed into the kitchen, threw her backpack on the bench, and ran to her room to get changed. When she came downstairs, she noticed her backpack was opened and on the floor.

Had someone moved it? Or did it fall over on its own?

Mona didn't stop to think; instead, she rushed into the backyard and went straight to the hidden grove. Making sure she was alone, she disappeared into the secret portion of their yard and stared glaringly at the tree with the bitter fruit.

True, Mona's first day of school wasn't nearly as bad as she had anticipated, with making a new friend and all, but still, she had hoped to get out of it entirely. Now? She was left with the repercussions of a strange tree growing in a secret portion of her family's woods. Maybe it wasn't a huge deal. If her parents found it, she could just tell them that it had been there all along…But should it even be alive to begin with? What if others found it and ate of its fruit? Or the animals? Surely something that bitter couldn't be good for anyone.

Mona couldn't help but feel responsible, the guilt of the unknown weighing heavily on her shoulders.

"Mone?" Lisa's voice echoed through the forest a little distance away. Lisa hadn't learned of this secret place, of that Mona was certain. If so, Lisa would have told her about it. She always had to share everything with Mona, no matter what it was. "Where are you? I saw you come out here…" Lisa's voice trailed off further away from Mona's hiding spot. Pretty soon, her voice went away altogether.

Apparently, now was not the best time to talk to the tree. At any moment, her sister might come back. And mona did *not* want Lisa to find her here.

"Don't think you're off the hook! I *will* have a word with you…soon…just not now," Mona whisper-shouted at the magic tree, glaring one last time at it before picking her way through the woods and into the backyard. She walked a short distance toward the house and stopped when she reached the hearty oak, the one she'd climbed the night of the seed planting, and breathed a sigh of relief. No one was around, or so she thought.

"There you are!"

Mona jumped, pulse quickening. Are people purposely

trying to frighten me today?

"Where were you?" Lisa's voice was unmistakably excited. "I looked everywhere!"

"Did you happen to look up?" Mona felt the lie escape her lips as she looked up at the oak. She blamed the untruth on her annoyance at being scared witless for the second time in one day.

"Well, no, I hadn't thought of it," Lisa answered, oblivious to Mona's attitude. "Actually, I came out here to ask you something." Lisa held up a brown paper bag for her sister to see.

Mona's cheeks heated, her pulse speeding up even more.

"Where did you find that?" Mona snatched the bag from out of Lisa's grip, opening it up to check on the remaining berries. "Did you go digging through my stuff? I've told you never to touch my things!"

"I was only curious! I saw you this morning in the car— you put something orange in there and I wanted to know what it was. I wouldn't have been as curious if *you* hadn't looked so sneaky." Lisa looked close to tears, clearly feeling bad for having done something to upset her sister. "I'm sorry, Mone."

Mona sighed. She couldn't remain angry at her sister for long. After all, Lisa was correct. Mona had been sneaky as of late, and the thought did little to ease her conscience. It seemed she had gotten into the habit of lying, but was it too risky to tell her sister the truth?

"It's all right, Leese. Next time, just ask, okay?"

"Okay." Lisa looked relieved. "So…what are they?" She wasted no time.

"Just something I'm working on," Mona began. Should she tell her? No, she would give it a few days. She still wanted time to figure out the tree's secrets on her own. "Nothing you need to be concerned about."

"I'm not concerned, Mona. I'm *curious*. You've never held secrets from me before, why now?" Lisa pouted, her arms crossed over her chest.

"You wouldn't understand," Mona began. "Besides, I don't have time to tell you. I have homework I need to get working on."

"Already? But it's only the first day!" Lisa argued.

"Yes, but you're not the one in seventh grade, I am," Mona countered as she brushed past her sister and entered the house.

She would talk to the tree later. Right now, she needed some time alone to collect her thoughts and dispose of the rest of these orange fruits. They were too nasty to eat and too risky to be seen.

But once she got to her room, Mona found she couldn't

seem to throw the last few away. Instead, she held them in her palm and studied them carefully.

Pollie's words came back to her: '*One bad apple ruins the bunch*!' Mona wondered if there were some Biblical truth to that…she hadn't read those exact words in the Bible anywhere. But what if there was no bunch to be ruined? The fruit hadn't been "bunched"' until they were put in her backpack…would that be enough time for one bad 'apple' to ruin the rest? Or was there something wrong with the tree?

Putting the berries aside, Mona decided she'd have to figure out the mystery another time. Right now, she needed to get some homework done.

As time ticked on, Mona completed a language arts assignment and started her algebra before making her way downstairs for dinner.

Her father had just walked through the doorway as Lisa was setting the oval dining table with plates and napkins. Her mother was taking a cooked chicken out of the oven, the steam wafting high and coiling against the oak cabinets and deep, cherry walls.

"Oh good, Mona you're here. I was just about to send Lisa to go get you." Her mother smiled warmly. "Please fill the glasses with everyone's drink preferences."

Mona complied, grabbing empty glasses from the

cupboard and getting drinks out of the fridge.

"How were your first days?" her father asked, setting his briefcase down and washing his hands. He went right to work on taking some silverware out of the drawer and helping Lisa with the table.

"It was excellent, Dad! I made so many friends, and I invited them to our house. Can they come over tomorrow after school? Please, pretty please?" Lisa begged, a huge smile on her face.

"Wow, that was quick! What did you do all day, chat?" her father joked, now helping Mona bring the filled glasses to the table.

"And learned! It was quite the industrious day."

"Industrious? Since when has your vocabulary become so sophisticated?" he jested.

"Since today, at precisely 1:00." Lisa smiled proudly.

"Well, I'm glad to see our taxpayer dollars are going to good use," her father remarked with a chuckle.

"Ted." Her mother's pleading tone was evidence enough that, though she found him humorous, she didn't want him to continue on that thread of conversation.

"Oh, I'm only messing around—now, what's this about your friends coming over?" He looked at Lisa.

"Can they? Tomorrow? Please?" she pleaded.

Mona's father and mother exchanged glances and the two nodded. "I don't see why we can't arrange that," he said with a smile. "I'm proud of you, sweetie, for making friends."

Mona didn't know why, but she felt the praise of his words slap her across the face. It wasn't that she wasn't happy for Lisa, but she hadn't been the one to make a friend group and invite anyone over. For some reason, that made her angry.

The table was finally set and all the food was brought out on potholders. They all took their seats and began to fill their plates with the steaming food. But before digging in, their father said grace.

"Thank you, Lord, for a home over our heads, provision on our table, and for a good education. You give us more than we deserve. Thank you that we can trust you in all things. Amen—dig in everybody!"

They all began to eat, and though Mona was hungry, she had little enthusiasm in lifting her fork. After her father's prayer, the idea of trust and truthfulness weighed heavily on her mind. How many lies were heaped upon her back now? Two? Five?

"And how was your day, Mona? Did you have a group of friends chasing you around the playground too?" Her father laughed, breaking through her thoughts.

Mona didn't want to answer but felt she had little choice.

"No. Seventh and eighth-graders don't get recess."

"The times have changed a lot since we've been in school, huh, Ellen?" Her father winked at his wife.

She looked bewildered and amused, "I *don't* want to talk about age tonight. Getting in and out of the car is enough to remind me I'm no spring chicken."

Her parents shared a collective chuckle before her father asked another question. "How was your day overall? Are you liking your classes?"

"Classes are good. I think math is going to be my favorite." Truthfully, the subjects weren't bad. It was just the social aspect, and math class seemed to provide the best option: less talking and more doing.

"Did you make any friends?" her father questioned.

"One," was all Mona replied.

"One is better than none, Mona. Regardless, I'm proud of you too." Her father smiled kindly.

Mona felt the guilt in her stomach grow. Would her father be proud to know all her lies? What about the tree? She hadn't told her parents the whole story.

Tomorrow morning before school, she'd talk to the tree again. She didn't want to risk another midnight escapade, and besides, she needed sleep.

Perhaps there was a way to make the tree disappear, to

send it on its way and make pretend none of this ever happened. If only.

Chapter 5

The Project

The next morning, Mona had no trouble waking up. She'd had a fitful night's sleep, tossing and turning and thinking about the conversation she'd yet to finish with that tree. She knew avoiding school was impossible at this point, but still, the tree was up to something. Or why else had it grown so fast just go produce the grossest fruit ever?

Mona quickly showered, dressed, and booked it downstairs before even her mother had finished getting ready. Mona wanted plenty of time to figure out the tree's secrets, especially since Lisa's friends would be over after school. Who knew what they'd be up to and if she'd even have time to sneak into the alcove without being seen.

She grabbed her backpack, laced up her shoes, and exited

the house. She practically sprinted through the woods to the hidden grove, ready to see the bright orange berries mocking her with their tantalizing secrets.

But upon seeing the tree, Mona was taken completely by surprise. The orange berries were gone, and in their place were bright turquoise fruits the size of peaches! The aroma encompassing the small enclosure was intoxicating and sickeningly delicious, making it hard for Mona to concentrate.

"What are you up to, tree?" she questioned, hands on her hips and scowling. Perhaps if she concentrated really hard, then the fruit's tempting smell wouldn't affect her brain so much. All she could think about was how they might taste.

But how on earth are they blue? Just yesterday they were orange! Not to mention their increase in size! Mona tried to steady her thoughts, challenging the tree to respond by scowling harder at its looming boughs.

But it didn't speak. It only swayed in the breeze, creaking under the slight pressure of the wind. Instead, it seemed to ignore her completely, only its fruit showing signs of interest as they glistened happily in the sun.

"Fine. Don't speak to me. But I have a feeling you're up to something. I made one wish and you've ruined it by growing into a bizarre fruit tree!" Mona stared at the sapling, scrutinizing it like she would a peculiar insect.

Finding nothing satisfactory, she plucked some of the turquoise fruits and stuffed them into her backpack. One way or another, she'd figure this tree out.

"Mona!" her mother's voice came echoing from the doorway and into the backyard. "Where are you, Mona?"

But it would have to wait. Right now, she had to get back inside, and besides, something told Mona that perhaps this tree had the upper hand. For even though she had been the one to plant it, it appeared to have a mind of its own.

Not to mention, she was still wondering if that strange cloud had anything to do with it. It really had looked like a ship…but it couldn't be. Ships didn't belong in the sky. Perhaps the magic *was* affecting her after all. Either that, or the tantalizing scent of fruit was making her addle-brained.

Planting the seed was turning out to be one of the biggest mistakes of her life.

What had she done?

* * *

At school, Mona found herself adjusting to her schedule; day two and she had remembered where all her classes were without getting lost.

Not to mention, Mona realized Pollie was in most of her

classes—that is, every class except Language Arts and Art. But four out of six wasn't bad. It was a stroke of luck that Mona happened to make friends with someone she spent most of her day with, and strangely enough, she was finding herself looking forward to her classes. Even lunch.

However, there was the slight issue of the fruit and lying to her only friend, not to mention her whole family. But how was Mona supposed to react if she didn't even understand it herself?

Mona plodded along from class to class, and she found herself losing concentration in Geography. The air smelled sickeningly sweet, almost as if honey and sugar were floating about the room in droves.

"Who is wearing perfume?" Mr. Frankweiler asked. "Girls, as much as it's preferable to smell nice, only a little dab should do. Not the entire bottle!" He walked over to a nearby window and let in some fresh air.

Mona looked down at her opened backpack and blanched. Instantly, she knew where the smell was coming from. Looking at the turquoise fruits staring back at her, it was as if they were mocking her very existence, their beauty and tantalizing smell sending the room into a catatonic frenzy. Quickly, she zipped the bag and tried to calm her racing heart. When she glanced at Pollie, she was eyeing Mona with a quizzical brow.

You okay? she mouthed with her lips.

I'm fine, Mona replied with her own, avoiding her friend's curious stares. But she wasn't fine, and she figured Pollie might see right through her. Yet another lie.

Once her bag was closed, it seemed the wafting fumes dissipated a little, still lingering in the air, but no longer infecting the room with their intoxicating smell.

Mona breathed a little easier. But this was far from over. Sooner or later, the fruit would be found out.

"Now class, as the fumes die down, let's resume our lesson on geographical regions of the world. If you would, take out your pens and study the maps before you..." Mr. Frankweiler said.

Mona stared at the flat parchment on her desk, a colorful array of shapes with names such as Europe, Australia, and South America staring back. There were so many words and so many places, but her eyes were drawn to the little orange-colored state labeled Arizona.

How I miss home.

"Okay, now that you've studied your maps, I would like you to circle at least three countries that are not the United States," Mr. Frankweiler said again. He walked around the room, watching students uncapping sharpies and pens, circling their countries, and staring back at him for instructions on what to do next.

"Great. Now, I'd like you to take a good look at what you've circled because those are going to be the three countries you're going to study and research on your own for the next three weeks."

There was a collective moan from the classroom and utterings of "I should have chosen that one instead!" or "I thought Wales was a mammal!" or even "Isn't Turkey a food?"

Mona looked back at her map and realized she had circled New Zealand, Scotland, and Egypt. It had been random, but she didn't know enough as to whether she should have chosen differently.

"And one more thing. You will be paired with at least two others in the class, and—Jeremy, Gretchen, hands down, I'll be picking partners," Mr. Frankweiler diverged. "As I was saying, you will be paired with two others, but they must have chosen different countries than your own. That way, amongst the three of you, you'll learn the cultures and customs of nine different places. I'll take a walk around the room now and take note of your choices, and then I'll call out group names from there."

Mona cast a worried glance at Pollie and tried to see

which places she had circled. From her vantage point, it looked like Pollie may have chosen something similar. Mona's heart plummeted. That would mean she'd have to work with new people.

"All right class." Mr. Frankweiler had a large pad of paper in his hand, his spectacles towards the edge of his nose. "I've determined your groups, and believe me, I'm just as excited as you are to get started."

The class groaned at his sarcastic statement.

"Gretchen, José, and Amber will be one group," Mr. Frankweiler began.

A cheer rang out from the two girls who high-fived while José rolled his eyes in exasperation. He clearly didn't want to be the only boy in the group.

"Alice, Thomas, and Bethany will be the next group," their teacher said. The group cheered quietly. Mr. Frankweiler continued to call out more names until only two groups were left to be formed.

Mona's palms were sweating. Between the six students, Pollie still hadn't been called which meant that perhaps they would be in a group together. But it was too soon to hope.

"Next is Phoebe, Marcus, and Paul," Mr. Frankweiler said and eyed Mona concernedly when she breathed out a huge sigh of relief.

Pollie hadn't chosen the same countries after all.

"And lastly, Pollie, Jeremy, and Mona," Mr. Frankweiler said, pointing to each of them in the process.

Mona turned to see a red-haired boy wave to her and Pollie from the back of the classroom. She guessed he must be Jeremy; he looked nice enough.

"Congratulations, class! You have just received your first group assignments. Here is the rubric." Mr. Frankweiler walked around the room and handed out the papers, a wide grin on his face. He clearly enjoyed torturing his students. "You will be graded on your individual research *and* your group presentations, so work wisely and work together. I suggest you exchange numbers and get to know one another."

Mona inwardly groaned as she half-listened to her teacher and skimmed over the rubric. This was sounding like a lot of work.

Mr. Frankweiler continued. "The main goal for these projects is for your group to compare and contrast all nine of your countries, highlighting their differences and similarities. Also keep in mind the importance of gathering reputable sources, citing those sources, and peer editing your research; your partners are supposed to help with that. And above all, a successful presentation will be built on honesty and trust: honesty for good communication and trust so you can depend on your partners to pull their weight so it doesn't affect your overall grade."

The bell to signal lunch had everyone jumping from their seats in surprise. But it was that last statement from her teacher which sent Mona's heart to beating wildly.

Chapter 6

A Web of Lies

Lunch was turning out to be more awkward than Mona had anticipated. Not only had Pollie's presence reminded Mona of her guilty conscience, but Pollie kept eying Mona's backpack as if she were waiting for an invitation.

"So, what's in the bag?" It seemed Pollie could no longer hold it in.

"Nothing." Mona lied, feeling the pit twist even deeper in her gut.

"Then why did you look so frightened in class?"

"I don't know what you're talking about." Mona quickly opened her backpack to pull out her lunch bag. She zipped it closed as fast as lightning before Pollie could peer inside. But in doing so, a strong whiff of something sweet circulated in the air.

"You do too know what I'm talking about, Mona! Why so secretive?" Pollie frowned, biting into her ham and cheese sandwich in aggravation. Her eyes searched Mona's for any sign of the truth, but Mona not knowing how to proceed, stared back in silence.

What could she say when she didn't understand it herself? It was one thing to have orange fruit—that was easier to explain. But turquoise? Pollie would know something was amiss, wouldn't she?

But as Mona continued to stare at Pollie, she could feel the hurt tangibly written across her face.

"Fine!" Mona dragged her backpack onto her lap and slowly opened it up. She reached inside and cautiously took out one of the fruits. The smell was even more pungent than before, but no one was close enough to their table to pay much attention. Pollie froze, her ham and cheese halfway to her mouth, gaping at the strange-looking produce.

"What *is* that?!" Pollie questioned excitedly.

"I'm not really sure." Mona shrugged.

"I've never seen anything like this before! Where'd you get it?"

"I um…my mom found them…" Mona couldn't believe how easy it was getting to lie. No matter how hard she tried, she wasn't ready to talk about the tree. She wanted to figure things out on her own. But how could keeping it a secret seem so wrong?

"Where? At a market from outer space?" Pollie reached over to poke at the fruit. "Is it edible?"

"I believe so, but I haven't tried this one yet. If it's anything like the orange ones from yesterday…" Mona shivered and let the unfinished sentence speak for itself. Truthfully, she was unsure whether the turquoise fruit would taste good or bad.

"Why don't we try it together?" Pollie suggested, her mouth salivating.

Mona felt her mouth doing the same. It *did* smell good. And it looked good, too. What could go wrong? Still, she was uncertain.

"I-I guess it's worth a shot," Mona replied.

The orange fruits had tasted nasty, but the girls had survived after eating them. Surely, it would be better with the turquoise ones. Right?

Mona's stomach knotted in anticipation as she reached into her backpack and pulled out a second fruit. She handed it to Pollie but was slightly hesitant. It felt risky sharing food she knew nothing about with someone she had just met. True, Pollie was becoming a fast friend, a friendship Mona could see lasting, but if something bad were to happen upon eating the fruit, how would she explain that to Pollie? How would Pollie ever forgive her?

On second thought, maybe it wasn't worth the risk.

"Actually, Pol—"

Too late. Pollie sunk her teeth into the blue skin before Mona had a chance to stop her. Mona choked back her words and watched in fear.

Pollie chewed for some time and swallowed. She grew thoughtful and was about to take a second bite but paused midway. Her face contorted into something of intense displeasure and she seemed to grow pale.

"Pollie?" Mona asked, her heart beating inside her chest like a bird trying to escape a gilded cage. "Are you okay?"

"I think I'm gonna be sick." Pollie got up and ran to the nearest trashcan, hurling into it with all her might.

Mona spent the rest of the school day accompanied by a pool of guilt as deep as the Marianas Trench.

* * *

The day only got worse when Mona was picked up from school. With all that had occurred throughout the day, she'd forgotten that Lisa was having friends over. Lisa: the younger sister, the one with the more manageable hair and smaller feet, the one who should be looking up to her older sister—this Lisa had already made five new friends. Mona felt that perhaps after today, she couldn't even count Pollie as her one.

"…And then we can continue our detective game in the woods! Samantha, you brought your magnifying glass, right?" Lisa turned around to address one of the three girls in the backseat.

"Yup! And Sofya brought her cipher journal!" It was evident that Samantha and Sofya were twins. The other three girls all looked different: one blonde with dimples, one brunette with mocha skin, and one auburn with freckles and green eyes.

"Excellent! Oh, this is going to be so much fun! Your parents aren't coming 'til after dinner, right?" Lisa asked all her friends, making sure there was enough time to hang out.

It was a unanimous 'yes' from all of them.

Mona couldn't help but feel the outsider, and this coming from being inside her own car! She noticed her mother giving her a curious look as they pulled into the garage while Lisa and her friends filtered out of the vehicle like fish in a stream.

"Thanks, Mrs. Ramone!" the girls all chimed together as they followed Lisa into the house.

Only the auburn-haired girl lingered behind, placing a

note in Mrs. Ramone's hand. "My dad wanted to thank you for having me over. Also, I have a food allergy, so this is just a note outlining some precautions if I go into anaphylactic shock," she said, smiling.

Mona's mother looked taken aback, but she recovered and just patted the girl's hand. "Thank you—"

"Ariel, ma'am," the girl replied.

"Well, thank you, Ariel. I will be sure to keep this close. Now why don't you meet up with your friends, I'm sure they're waiting for you." Her mother smiled.

The girl nodded and bolted from the car, her backpack hanging haphazardly from one shoulder.

"I feel like she thinks I'm the school nurse or something." Her mother chuckled to herself and then looked to Mona, her smile turning more serious.

Mona made to follow after them, but her mom steadied her with a gentle hand on her arm.

"Mona, I know it's only your second day, but something seems off. Are you sure you're okay?"

"I'm fine." Mona lied, not feeling like going into detail about her day nor the turmoil she felt inside.

"Okay, but I'm always here to talk to. You know that, right?" her mother asked.

"I know." Mona gave her mother a reassuring smile she

didn't feel before grabbing her backpack and leaving the car. The sounds of Lisa and her friends giggling reached her ears as she walked inside the house. Mona rolled her eyes.

"Hey, Mone, you wanna play with us?" Lisa questioned.

Mona could tell it was sincere, but the thought of hanging out with a bunch of fifth-graders made her feel even angrier. Instead of replying, Mona just hugged her backpack tighter and trudged up the stairs, the sounds of Lisa and her friends' voices fading in the distance as they made their way outside.

Mona entered her room and shut the door behind her. She threw her backpack on the ground and fell backward onto her bed in an exasperated huff. Staring at the ceiling, she realized she was more exhausted than she had been in weeks. Sure, the school year had just started and this was only day two of homework, but it was more than that. She wasn't just doing schoolwork; she was harboring secrets. And not only had she just ignored her sister, she still hadn't found out how Pollie had recovered from eating that fruit.

"Pollie!" Only just remembering, Mona was up and scrambling for her Geography notebook. She'd written her number down somewhere. Digging through her backpack, she dislodged some of the turquoise fruits as they tumbled to the floor, but Mona ignored them as she pulled the journal out and turned through its pages. There! Pollie's neat handwriting showcased her seven-digit number alongside Jeremy's chicken-scratched one. She never understood how boys got anything done with handwriting like that.

Mona quickly ran to the hallway to grab the house phone off the table. Her rapid movements almost knocked over the fresh vase of flowers her mother had put there after church on Sunday. Almost, but not quite, as the vase teetered back and forth before righting itself next to the receiver.

She rushed back to her room and shut the door behind her. Mona was about to dial the number when the phone began ringing in her hands.

"You've got to be kidding me," she moaned under her breath. Not recognizing the number, she almost didn't answer it. But seeing as she could just hang up if the person was a telemarketer or someone asking for money, Mona took her chances.

"Hello?" Mona questioned.

"Mona? Is that you?" The voice came over the other line.

"Pollie? Oh my goodness, how are you feeling? I was just about to call you!" Mona was completely shocked.

"Hey Mona, I thought I'd be able to reach you on here. I wanted to let you know I'm feeling a lot better and not to blame yourself for what happened," Pollie began.

Mona didn't know what to say, so she just remained quiet

while Pollie continued to talk.

"When I told my mom about the strange fruit and the orange one from the day before, she got really concerned. I told her it wasn't your fault since you didn't know where they were from, but she is concerned with why your mom would buy them in the first place. Basically, I'm calling because my mom wants to talk to your mom."

Mona's blood ran cold. Pollie's mom wanted to talk to *her* mom? How could this be happening? She had to do something, but what?

All of a sudden, there was a loud knock on her bedroom door. Mona panicked and dropped the phone as Lisa opened the door, cautiously poking her head inside.

"Hey Mone, sorry to interrupt…but I figured you might know the answer. What is this?" In one of Lisa's hands was a bright, turquoise fruit.

Chapter 7

When Truth Comes Knocking

It was all happening too fast and all at once. Mona's world was crashing down around her.

She stared at Lisa standing in the doorway. Her sister's eyes darted from Mona to the phone on the bed, and then to the turquoise fruits on the floor.

"What are you hiding—?"

"Get out, brat!" Mona got up and pushed her sister through the doorframe and slammed the door shut.

Mona's heart pounded wildly against her ribs as she pressed her back firmly against the door. She stared at the phone lying on her bed, taunting her with unresolved problems. How was she supposed to get out of this?

She pushed herself forward and gingerly grabbed the

phone. Pollie's voice sounded through the receiver without it even having touched Mona's ear.

"Hello? Mona? What's going on?" Pollie's tone rang with concern.

Mona swallowed and placed the phone to her mouth. "Sorry, Pollie, that was my sister come to wreak havoc on my life…"

"Is everything okay?"

"Everything's fine!" The guilt twisted even sharper in Mona's gut.

"Well, is your mom there?" Pollie's voice shrank to a whisper. "Mine's been breathing down my neck for the past five minutes…"

"Uh, um…my mom's not home at the moment." Mona was sure the lie could be heard through the phone. Her mom was, in fact, downstairs and was probably on her way upstairs now after how Mona had just treated Lisa. Mona only had so much time.

"Do you know when she'll be back?" Pollie questioned.

"I—"

"Mona!" Her mother's voice carried from somewhere downstairs. Her footsteps sounded on the stairs as they came closer.

"I have to go." Mona's hands grew clammy on the phone,

her heart tumbling like an acrobat inside her chest.

"But how will…" Pollie's voice droned on.

"Mona! Open this door right now!" Her mom was on the other side of her door, her tone anything but pleasant. "Don't make me come in there!"

"Mona, who is that?" Pollie asked.

"Three." Her mom's countdown had begun. Mona hated when it came to this.

"Uh, no one. I need to…" Mona paused midsentence, eyeing the blue fruits still scattered about the floor. Her mom would see them if she came into the room!

"Two." The doorknob twisted slightly. In the next second the door would fly open.

Mona threw the phone onto the bed and frantically started collecting the blue fruits, stuffing them into her trashcan.

"One." Her mom burst through the door, hands on her hips and a scowl on her face. "What on earth do you think you're doing? And why does it smell like a fruit basket in here?"

Mona sat on the edge of her bed, fidgeting with the folds of her shirt as she tried to steady her racing heart. She opened her mouth to respond but found it was dry. She forgot about the fruit's scent! Of course, their pungent smell would permeate her small room…

"Did you hear me, Mona? What do you think you're doing? I get it if you don't want to talk to me, but you just slammed the door in your sister's face! That needs explaining. This isn't like you." Her mom crossed the room to open a window before she stood in front of the door once more, crossing her arms over her chest, frowning.

Lisa was a notorious tattletale. Why couldn't she just mind her own business and leave Mona alone?

"I…I don't know." Everything in Mona wanted to tell the truth, but she was already in so deep. How would she get out of it now?

A thought suddenly hit her. Had Lisa told their mom about the blue fruit? Showed her the tree? She swallowed hard at the thought.

"Well, I hope you're comfortable because you'll be spending the remainder of the night in your room. I'll bring dinner up when it's time to eat, and maybe by then you'll be ready to talk." Her mom stepped closer to the bed and reached behind Mona.

Mona blanched when her mom grabbed hold of the phone—wishing, hoping, praying—that Pollie wasn't still on the other line. In her haste to gather the turquoise fruit off the floor, she'd forgotten to hang up on her friend.

"And no more phone. Whoever you were talking to can

wait until tomorrow. Is that clear?" Her mom arched her brows.

"Yes." Mona nodded and heard the telltale beep of the off button when her mother hung up the phone. Had it been on this whole time or was the action just precautionary? Either way, Mona breathed a sigh of relief. Pollie wouldn't learn the truth tonight.

"Hopefully, some time alone will help you think up a suitable apology to your sister. I'm sure she's expecting one." Her mother grabbed the doorknob and was halfway through the door before she stopped and turned around. "I say all of this because I love you, Mona. And I expect more from you, as I'm sure you do yourself. Know that I'll be updating your father on everything when he gets home." She closed the door and her footsteps could be heard shuffling along the carpet in the hallway.

Mona fell backward on her bed for the second time that night and let out a huge sigh. Tears stung the corners of her eyes and the seed of guilt in her stomach sprouted new roots. How could all this be happening? How could not wanting to go to school have caused all these problems?

It was that stupid seed. And now the tree was mocking her with its crazy fruit. She wanted nothing more than to chop it down and use its logs as fuel for a fire. Its only purpose was to cause trouble.

Mona sat up and grabbed her backpack, fishing out her homework. Anything to distract her mind from her problems.

She had grabbed a few books from the school library for her Geography project: two books on Egypt, one on Scotland, and two on New Zealand. She took them out and laid them across her bed. Next, she took out her Geography folder and found her graphic organizers for the countries.

She might as well get going on this project; Jeremy had mentioned he'd get started on his portion tonight so he could share his findings tomorrow. Mona felt compelled to do the same. Was Pollie working on hers now too? The thought that all three of them might be working on their project at the same time, despite the distance, helped her feel less alone.

It was a small thing, but it did feel good to be productive after having disappointed her family. If she was lucky, maybe she'd even get enough done so tomorrow she'd have more time to smooth things over with Pollie.

* * *

The sound of the doorbell shook Mona from her work. She glanced at the clock on her nightstand and saw that it was already 5:00 pm. She'd worked hard for two hours straight.

But who could be at the door?

Were Lisa's friends going home already? No…they were staying for dinner. And seeing as Mona hadn't been given any food, she assumed dinner hadn't happened yet. Then who was at the door?

Mona was paranoid. Normally this wouldn't bother her so much, but seeing as the day's events kept spiraling more and more out of control, she couldn't help but worry.

She edged closer to her door and twisted the knob. Pulling it open a crack, she peered out. The sound of voices engaged in conversation floated over the banisters.

Her mother was talking to a woman, and it was getting heated. But Mona found that the voices weren't necessarily heated toward each other. No, they were upset about something else. Who was her mother talking to?

The voices became clearer and Mona found they were talking about her. Her mother said her name. No—more like yelled it.

"Mona Jayne Ramone!" her tone was filled with aggravation. "Come down here, please!"

Mona's heart picked up its pace once more, and she found her fingers grow slick on the doorknob. Her breath hitched in her throat and her stomach plummeted like a falcon to its prey. What was going on?

Each step down the stairs felt like she was walking to her doom. Immediately she had flashbacks to the first day of school where she had felt the same way about walking to her homeroom. But this time was different. This time, she *was* in trouble.

As Mona reached the bottom steps, she paused. Standing in the foyer of their home was a dark-haired woman with glasses and a strong jaw. She was dressed in work clothes and pointed stilettos with a black pocketbook strung over one shoulder.

And behind her stood Pollie.

Chapter 8

From Seed to Soil

"Pollie? What are you doing here?" Mona swallowed hard and her hands fidgeted with the hem of her shirt. Deep down Mona knew the reason for her friend's visit, but she didn't want to admit that. Perhaps there was another reason.

Pollie didn't say anything; she just glanced at the floor while her mother turned an angry gaze toward Mona.

Her eyes narrowed and her grip tightened on her pocketbook strap.

Mona's mother turned to face her daughter as well. Having two furious women staring at Mona was doing strange things to her stomach.

"Mona, Mrs. Archibald is here with a serious concern about something you said *I* played a part in." If it was possible, the scowl on her mother's face went even deeper. "She mentioned something about fruit—colorful fruit—that you said I'd bought at the store. What's this all about?"

"I, uh…" Mona's hands ceased their fidgeting, her fingers numb with fear. It was happening. The truth was unraveling like a ribbon around her feet. But where to start?

"Your daughter *poisoned* my daughter!" Mrs. Archibald sneered at Mona, standing up straighter in the process.

"Now wait just a minute…" Mona's mother whirled around to face Mrs. Archibald, shielding Mona from most of her acrimony. "I don't know what's going on, but she didn't *poison* anybody!"

"I-I didn't mean to, honest! I can explain." Mona looked from behind her angry mother to their even angrier visitor.

"Whatever happened, I'm sure you didn't mean to, Mona." Her mother came to her defense and turned to face her again, the moment of reprieve lasting all of two seconds. "But that still doesn't tell me what's going on…"

Pollie's gaze lingered on the floor; she shifted her weight uncomfortably from one foot to the other.

"Well…?" Mrs. Archibald arched her brows and asked expectantly, eyeing Mona with an intensity like an erupting volcano.

"I…" Mona's mouth suddenly felt dry as if she hadn't

tasted water in weeks. And was that her eye twitching? She swallowed hard and tried to think of some sort of explanation to make sense of this whole thing. But it was too confusing. Perhaps it was time for the truth. "I found a seed."

"A seed? What kind of seed?" Her mother's brow furrowed in confusion, contrasting Mrs. Archibald's whose eyes widened with sudden apprehension.

Pollie glanced up, her expression hard to read.

Mona gulped, her heart rate increasing. "I found it in the woods behind our house. I…I can't even explain how I found it. It was like it had found me."

The more Mona thought about it, it was strange how she'd found the seed in the first place. She hadn't known it was special at the time; she hadn't even known what to look for. But when her eyes had alighted on the odd, silvery object in the hidden alcove, and when her fingers had fastened around it, she'd hoped it was of the magical sort. The ship cloud hovering above the grove felt even more proof of that, though she didn't know what it all meant. In the grove, the air had pulsed with an odd feeling; Mona had wondered if it was her fear or if it was the magic she was hoping for. Perhaps it was a mixture of both, though, at the time, she had doubted the latter.

She knew better now. The magic *was* real, but what sort

of magic was it? Good or bad?

"Mona, what does a seed have to do with anything?" her mother questioned, arms now crossed over her chest.

"This is gonna sound so stupid." Mona groaned. She didn't want to explain how her imagination had gotten the best of her yet again. She was known for her dreaming and adventuring, always spinning wild tales of talking beasts and flitting faeries to her sister. Her parents had thought it was cute when she was younger, but what would they think now?

"It's not stupid, Mona. Every explanation has to start somewhere," her mother urged her on, waiting.

Mona nodded and began. "I didn't want to go to the new school." That part sounded normal, but she hesitated to say the next words; they sounded so foolish to her own ears. She took a steadying breath and proceeded, trying to sound as grown-up as possible. "I was desperate to find a way out and wished for something, like a beanstalk or a fantastical realm, so I could climb and disappear. When I found the seed, I didn't *actually* think it would work, though I had serious hopes it would…" Mona tugged on her hair, feeling even more ridiculous than ever.

"What happened to that seed, Mona?" her mother asked.

"I…I planted it. Late one night in the woods. The next day it had grown into a giant tree. That's how I knew the seed was magical. It takes years for trees to grow, anyone knows that." Mona swallowed and began to fidget with the ring on her finger, twisting it in circles. "When I saw the tree for the first time, I was shocked it had grown at all and disappointed it hadn't turned into a magic beanstalk—there would be no escaping school. But there were odd orange fruits hanging from its branches."

"I remember those! They tasted awful too," Pollie finally chimed in, her lips pulled into a slight frown.

"Yeah, they were disgusting. But I hadn't known how to explain them. And when the fruit turned blue the following day, I felt I had even less of a clue how to explain what happened." Mona looked up and met Pollie's gaze. "Pollie, I'm so sorry, I should have told you the truth."

Mona's mother cinched her brow into a concerned scowl. "I don't quite know how to respond to this whole magic business, but I'm shocked. You lied to us and your friend and blamed all of this on your own mother. You both could have gotten seriously ill!" She shook her head in displeasure. And then something seemed to click as her expression grew thoughtful. "I'm assuming this explains the fruit smell I found in your room, then." It was more a statement than anything.

Mona only nodded; her words stuck to her tongue.

"*My* daughter *did* get ill! She threw up! What's next?

Tomorrow's fruit causing hospitalization?" Mrs. Archibald scolded and grew even more serious. She then turned to Mona. "Tell me what this seed looked like!"

Mona felt like a fish who was being speared by Mrs. Archibald's piercing glare. "Uh…um, it was hairy and shiny silver. I'd never seen anything like it before."

The words seemed to affect Mrs. Archibald; her glare now turned into fixed horror. Her eyes went wide, and her hands began to tremble unsteadily like she had experienced something before that she didn't want to relive. "This is all ridiculous! Sounds like black magic to me. I've had enough of this idiocy—come on, Pollie. We're going home." She spun on her high heels, fear burning in her eyes as she reached the door. She twisted the gold doorknob and turned to see her daughter still standing where she was, eyes shifting from the floor to Mona. "Now, Pollie."

"Mona…" Pollie looked like she wanted to speak, but the words stopped before they came out. Instead, she turned to follow her mom out the door.

"I'm so sorry, Pollie." Mona's heart cracked. She was losing her only friend over a stupid tree. Over stupid fruit. Why had lying caused all of this? Would Pollie ever want to speak to her again?

The door clicked shut behind their visitors, and the silence lingering in their absence could be cut with a knife.

Never had such tension made Mona want to rip her hair out as much as it did now. She could feel her mother's eyes on her profile, studying her closely.

"Mona." Her voice was short.

Mona turned to face her mother, afraid of the consequences. How could she have done things differently? She wished she'd never found the seed at all.

"You have some explaining to do. But first, if you're telling the truth like I hope you are, you need to show me this tree."

The coldness from her mother's voice wound its way into Mona's middle, suffocating her steady flow of oxygen. She was in trouble. Big time.

Mona nodded. "Follow me." For the third time in one week, she felt like she was walking to her doom.

* * *

Dinner that night was awkward and lackluster. Mona could tell her mother felt guilty for serving Lisa's friends microwavable dinners rather than a homecooked meal, but with Mrs. Archibald and Pollie, not to mention the tree, taking up most of the night, dinner had been rushed and hastily thrown together.

And Mona was hastily thrown back into her bedroom. She would probably be locked away in there for the foreseeable future, getting nightly dinners brought to her door like a prisoner to her cell.

This was only the beginning.

After dinner, her mother said she was going to have a stern talk with Mona. And her father would be joining them as well.

Mona slurped up some weak noodles, pushing them around with the tip of her fork. Homework forgotten and sprawled across her bed, she felt anything but motivated to finish what she had started.

It was nearing 6:00, and the sounds of cars turning their engines, accompanied by slamming doors, reached her ears. Lisa's friends were going home, and that meant one step closer to Mona receiving her punishment.

By the time her reheated meal had congealed to the bottom of the dish, Mona heard footsteps trudge up the stairs, low voices murmuring in displeased tones.

"...I've seen it with my own eyes, Ted! What are we going to do? All this talk of magic is unsettling. It can't be good to have that mysterious thing growing in our backyard doing who-knows-what to the animals and unsuspecting people. It's dangerous!" Her mother's voice could be heard through the other side of the door.

"Ellen, honey, it's only a tree. It's easy to manage. Right now, I think we had better focus on the bigger issue at hand: our daughter's incessant lying," Mona's father said, a shortness and gentleness to his words.

Mona could hear her mother sigh. "You're right. There's no use worrying. Are you ready to talk to her?"

Mona's father must have nodded for the voices stopped outside her door and the sound of the doorknob twisting indicated that her prison cell was now receiving visitors. What would be her punishment?

Her parents came into her bedroom and closed the door behind them. They each took a seat in front of the door, one on her desk chair and the other on a nearby cushion. Mona sat on her bed, awaiting her fate.

"Let's start with the lying, Mona." Her father leaned forward in his chair and interlocked his fingers as he rested his elbows on his knees. The look in his eyes belayed disappointment mixed with hurt.

"I never meant to lie," Mona uttered, feeling the space behind her eye twitch again. "It sorta just happened. I hadn't wanted to go to school, so I planted a seed...I never thought it'd actually work..." The guilt twisted like a knife in her gut.

"It's a serious thing to lie, Mona. There are serious consequences, you know that," her father said, taking a deep breath.

Mona nodded.

"And your sister only wanted the truth. She hadn't told anyone anything until your mother saw that she was crying. And then when Mrs. Archibald came over…." Her father ran a hand over his face. "What were you thinking, Mona?"

"Apparently I wasn't." Mona let herself wallow in her guilt, the emotion making her eyes sting with tears.

"Honey, we want what's best for you. Why didn't you want to go to school?" It was her mother's turn to ask a question now.

"Because I liked Arizona, Mom. I didn't want to come here at all." She could tell the truth of her words stung both her parents.

"Change isn't always a bad thing, sweetie," her father said.

"It is when you leave your friends behind to start the seventh grade in a completely new school!" It was Mona's turn to raise her voice. She was undone, completely raw and vulnerable now.

"I know it must be hard for you, honey, but your father's new job meant a great opportunity for us as a family. And you

weren't alone in starting everything over again, Lisa did too—
"

"You don't get it! She started in the *fifth* grade! Do you know how many new kids enter fifth grade? About half! And do you know how many new kids enter the seventh grade? Hardly any! She's already gotten a leg up on me, Mom, and now I think I've lost my only friend…" Mona trailed off, her breath heaving. When had she swallowed that lump of air? It felt like a rock was trying to dissolve in her chest, the pressure making her lightheaded and shaky.

"We had no idea this was how you were feeling, Mona. I'm sorry my job has caused this much pain for you." Her father frowned. "But if this is how you respond in times of change and discomfort, you're on a troublesome road. Do you understand?"

Mona finally swallowed past the lump in her throat. Her shirt felt sticky on her skin as if she had just sweated out all her nerves. She nodded. "I do now." Why hadn't she used her brain earlier?

"I'm afraid there will be consequences." Her father resumed his position with fingers interlocked and elbows on his knees.

Mona could only guess what these consequences entailed. Grounded from school? Grounded from talking to her only friend? Grounded from the dinner table?

"You'll be going to school like usual, but whenever you're home, you're grounded," her father said.

Mona released a nervous sigh. That wasn't so bad.

"There's more. That tree of yours is nothing but trouble. But I feel as though simply tearing it down will defeat the purpose of the lesson. You are to take care of it every day until your grounded period is up. That tree is in your care for a month."

Mona's heart sank. An entire month? How was she supposed to take care of that monstrous thing that only caused her trouble? Little good it ever did for her.

"You will prune it. You will water it. You will pick all its fruit and toss it out. You will do whatever it takes to keep it beautiful and thriving, and you will not hide it any longer. Do I make myself clear?"

Mona swallowed hard. "Perfectly."

"Good." Her father moved to stand and bent down to kiss Mona atop her head. "This will be good for you. There's a good lesson in it."

Her mother moved to do the same, and before Mona knew it, both of them had bid her goodnight and left her room.

She was all alone with her impending duty looming over her shoulders.

From seed to soil, this task would be her undoing.

How she longed for Arizona. How she longed for things to be back to normal. How she longed for that tree to just disappear entirely.

Chapter 9

Pruning

Waking up for school the following morning felt like walking through a tub of molasses, slow and murky.

Mona had spent a good portion of the night crying herself to sleep—her lies haunting her dreams, the looks on the faces of those she hurt—so much so that now her eyes were puffy and swollen.

When she looked in the bathroom mirror it was to her horror at what stared back. The bags under her eyes were large and were probably still swollen from hiding what felt like a month's worth of secrets inside them.

She massaged the skin, splashed water on her face, and begrudgingly dressed in the first outfit she saw. She grabbed her backpack and trudged down the stairs.

The third day of school. Day one of being grounded. Only twenty-seven days left to go…

When Mona rounded the banister, Lisa's happy and sunshiny face looked up at her from the kitchen counter, a pop tart in her hand. Lisa's smile quickly faded and was replaced with a frown as she turned her back on Mona. The bites to her pop tart were now short and rigid like she was taking out her feelings on the food itself.

Mona brushed past her sister into the kitchen to grab a breakfast bar. She only stayed long enough to peel the wrapper off and throw it in the trash before she made her way out the garage door.

She could feel Lisa's eyes on her back, but the last thing Mona wanted to do right now was apologize. It was what Lisa was expecting, but Mona didn't want to give her the satisfaction. There was already too much tormenting her mind, and she didn't need Lisa's perfect, smiling face reminding her of just how far she'd fallen.

Mona wanted to forget any of this happened. That's why she was heading straight for the car. She'd sit in the front seat all morning if it meant she didn't have to face the tree, her sister, or Pollie at school.

Pollie. Mona swallowed a bite of her breakfast bar, nearly choking as the food went down hard.

She hadn't considered how going to school would be ten times worse now than it had been only a few days ago. It hadn't even been a full week and she'd made an enemy. Or at least an enemy to her only friend's mom. But when you're in the seventh grade, it's basically the same thing.

Mona opened the door of the white minivan and threw her backpack on the ground. She threw herself in the same way and sat. Waiting.

The terror of the day would come soon enough.

* * *

Sitting in Language Arts was a balm before the impending tempest. This was one of the two classes Pollie wasn't in, and if Mona was lucky, maybe Pollie wouldn't be in school today.

Mona sat in her chair listening to her teacher drone on about Greek mythology and the Trojan Horse.

"…You see, class, the Greeks pretended to leave the battle and appease Athena, the goddess of war, by giving a large, wooden horse to the people of Troy. But all of them were deceived. For this horse would allow the Greeks to gain entry into the gated city without anyone being the wiser."

"Mrs. Barthold, I have a question." A blonde-haired boy with glasses raised his hand.

"Felix, I thought we've been over this already. When you raise your hand, that does not mean you *also* need to call out with your voice. I *do* have eyes you know." Mrs. Barthold sighed and adjusted her glasses to prove her point even further. "Now, what is your question?"

"So, the Greek people lied to enter Troy, right? They got what they wanted through deception, but how did it end?" Felix questioned.

"If you would've listened but a moment longer, your question would be answered by now." Mrs. Barthold sighed again and walked to the front of the room where a picture of the Trojan Horse was projected onto the board.

"Now class…" Mrs. Barthold began but was soon cut off by the blaring of a bell.

Class was over.

Mrs. Barthold, clearly frustrated by having her lesson interrupted before she could finish, quickly administered the homework. "Don't forget I want those five-paragraph essays on a Greek myth of your choosing by Monday next week. It's already Wednesday, so plan accordingly!" She was practically screaming the instructions out the door.

While everyone filed out of class, Mona lingered behind, slowly making efforts to leave the room.

What if Pollie shows up in Algebra I? The idea made

Mona wish she were glued to her seat.

Mrs. Barthold turned sharply from the doorway, muttering under her breath, "That infuriating child, I'd box his ears if I was allowed…" She blanched and startled at seeing Mona still sitting in her seat; her hand flew to her chest, her eyes wide. "Good Heavens, I didn't see you there!" It was evident that she had undergone quite the shock at being overheard. She tried smoothing her features along with her dress as she begged a question, "Is everything all right, Ms. Ramone?"

For some reason, seeing her teacher get flustered and having a window into her unkind thoughts, sent a wave of ease into Mona's gut. *No one is perfect.* The thought made her feel lighter, if by a degree.

"Yes, I'm just leaving now." Mona bent to grab her backpack and slowly made for the door. She'd have to go to Algebra one way or another, and eventually, she'd have to make it through this day…not to mention all of the seventh grade.

What's the worst that could happen?

* * *

Mona was outside trying to avoid the branches falling on her head. Her pruning shears were in one hand while the other held fast to the trunk. Her right foot was up on a limb while her left toe pressed ever so gently on the ladder below; her father had delivered it to the grove early that morning before he left for work.

She'd been outside tending to the tree ever since she got home. It was better to do the deed in the daylight, and besides, it was a good distraction from how awful her day at school had gone.

Pollie had shown up for all her classes, but she never once looked over at Mona. Or at least she hadn't looked over anytime Mona was looking. Still, the silence spoke louder than words. Their friendship was as good as dead.

Now Mona was busily cutting away at the dead parts of the tree, dropping the strange-looking fruits onto the ground from above in the process. Today's were a bright, cherry red and they were shaped like a softball. Mona didn't even think twice about tasting one. She knew better.

Mona climbed even higher and tried to reach the topmost branches when her foot slipped and knocked the ladder over. Now she was stuck. She looked down and saw the metal rungs had smushed some of the cherry fruits into the ground; their disturbingly sweet odor wafted high into the boughs. It looked like a massacre, and Mona didn't want her own blood to mingle amongst the fruits if she fell the wrong way.

"Help!" Mona cried. She felt foolish, but already the sun was beginning to set and she had homework to do. True, she wasn't too high up and could get down if she maneuvered herself carefully, but she'd rather have the ladder. It would be faster, and she needed time to clean up all this mess. "Help!" she shouted one more time.

She heard someone coming. Mona was certain her mother would've heard her through the kitchen window. Sure enough, the sound of footsteps shuffling over leaves drew nearer.

"Mone?" The voice belonged to her sister. Someone Mona wanted nothing to do with. At least not today.

Lisa stepped out from the woods and now stood in the clearing, looking up into the tree. She crossed her arms and frowned. "Are you okay?" By the look on her face, it appeared talking to Mona wasn't something she wanted to do either.

"I'm fine. Can you just get the ladder up for me?" Mona asked, eager to get down from this tree. She eyed a lower branch that she could grab ahold of and climb to the ground if necessary, but the thought made her nervous. If she could just get the ladder back…She'd done enough pruning for one day, and besides, the tree would still be here tomorrow. Heck, she had the whole month to finish keeping this thing alive and healthy.

"Depends." Lisa bit her lip and dug the toe of her left foot into the ground. She picked up a red fruit in the process, eyeing it carefully.

"Depends on what?" Mona quirked a brow, not liking the sound of how this was going.

"If I do something nice for you, you can't be mean to me for an entire week," Lisa suggested, dropping the fruit before crossing her arms.

Mona's heart dropped. It had come to this…her sister was practically begging for Mona to be nice to her. When had she become so calloused?

At that moment, Mona hated the tree with everything in her. She hated it so much she wanted to stomp it back into the ground.

She picked her foot up and started stomping on the branch, not even caring that she was probably hurting it or that she might accidentally hurt herself. She wanted this thing gone. It had ruined her life and was continuing to haunt her.

"I'll take that as a no." Lisa looked up with tears in her eyes, her frown even deeper. She quickly turned around and started to leave.

Before Mona even had a chance to realize what was happening, Lisa was already gone.

"Wait, Leese!"

But she never came back.

Chapter 10

Mona Lisa

It was uncomfortable eating dinner with her family. Uncomfortable because the conversation seemed to drift over and around Mona, but never toward her. She wasn't necessarily taking strides to be engaging, either; she cast her gaze on her plate whenever Lisa looked her way. The tension was as thick as fog.

After dinner, Mona trudged up the stairs to her room. She was to be confined to the four beige-painted walls within, and all without a phone, computer, or anything electronic for a month. If she had to type a paper or do research for any reason, she *was* allotted an hour per day on the computer with strict boundaries on websites, so she had to use her time wisely.

Since Mona had a paper for Language Arts due Monday

and a Geography project due in a few weeks, she decided to use some computer time now. She was studiously working away when a knock sounded on her door.

Her father poked his head in. "Are you busy?"

"I'm just working on some homework," Mona replied, barely looking up from the screen as her fingers typed furiously at the keys.

"Can you put that aside for a few minutes? I'd like to talk for a bit." Her father entered the room and took a seat at her desk chair. He ran his hand over his chin before he rested his elbows on his knees and laced his fingers together.

For the longest time, this was how her father had always talked to her. He always leaned forward with a pinched brow, looking as if what he had to say pained him more than how it would pain the listener. And his fingers were always interlaced while his elbows rested on his knees. His classic pose.

And this time was no different.

"Do you remember the story of how you got your name?" her father questioned.

Mona thought back. Something about visiting another country and croissants came to mind. In truth, she'd been so young and hadn't paid much attention to all the details. "Not really." She shrugged, biting her lip.

Her father nodded. "I'll tell you another little story first." He cleared his throat before beginning. "You know, when I was growing up, I always loved art history."

Art history? What did that have to do with anything? Her father must have been one weird kid…

"I loved traveling the world with your grandmother, going to art galleries, and visiting castles. Gran always had an eye for color and talent, as I'm sure you recall. She'd take me to someplace new nearly every week. Sometimes Charlie, my younger brother, would join us, which I was never happy about." Her father creased his forehead and rubbed the back of his neck in irritation before continuing, "We hadn't always gotten along as kids, which you already know…Thankfully, it was mostly just Gran and me, marveling at what people created with their own two hands." Her father paused and looked around her room.

"That painting of Big Ben above your bed was painted by your grandmother, years ago. It never hung in an art gallery, but I thought it should have. I wanted to see it there someday, and as a young boy, I thought I would."

Mona looked at the painting and nodded in agreement. There was something special about the way the light hit it just right during certain times of the day as if silver dust danced around the clock in magic swirls.

"One summer, Gran decided to surprise me with a two-week trip to Europe. We went all over the U.K. and France, visiting countless castles and museums, but the crown jewel of the trip was seeing both the Eiffel Tower and Big Ben in person. Since watching *Peter Pan* as a kid, that giant clock always had me mesmerized." He looked at the painting once more and smiled as if in memory. "In truth, both structures were spectacular and sights not much has ever compared to 'til this day, except seeing your mother on our wedding day and when both you and Lisa were born. I shall never forget those moments amidst all the memories in the world." He paused a moment. "But there was something else on that trip that stole my breath in a different way. We went to the Louvre in Paris, France, the world's largest art museum, and what do you think we saw?"

"Uh…art?" Mona felt her cheeks blush at how ridiculous she sounded.

Her father laughed. "Indeed, we did. And plenty of it. But it was something small and unassuming that got my complete attention. The portrait of a woman."

"A woman?" Mona quirked a brow, trying to remember this detail in the story. It was all rather fuzzy.

"Yes, she had this look about her which was almost unreadable. Was she happy? Pensive? Hurting? Smug?

Naturally, as an observer at the age of thirteen, I thought maybe at the time she was suffering from too much gas." Her father laughed and shook his head.

"Dad!" Mona laughed in response.

"You can't fault the lack of maturity in a teenage boy, Mona. Believe me, it's produced in spades in all of us." Her father chuckled once more and then grew serious. "Gran was quick to inform me of the portrait's creator as Leonardo DaVinci, one of the greats! Have you heard of him?"

Mona nodded. She'd learned about the painter at some point in school back in Arizona.

"He painted many beautiful things, but this was one of his most famous pieces. As a young boy, the weight of it didn't sink in, but over the years, I took the memory of the portrait with me, carrying its image into adulthood and my career. And do you remember what the title of the portrait is called?"

Mona thought to herself, mulling over the possibilities. Try as she might, she couldn't think of it. What was the lady's name? "I don't remember."

"Mona Lisa," her father said.

"Oh yeah!" Mona was excited to finally have the memory of the name return, but the gravity of it didn't hit until a few seconds later. "Wait…"

Her father smiled. "Yes, the Mona Lisa, one woman with

two names that just so happens to be yours and your sister's."

The light seemed to dawn even more. She and Lisa were named after a famous painting, one of the most famous paintings in the world. For some reason, she knew she'd never forget this story again. But why had her father reshared it?

"Listen, Mona, I couldn't help but notice you and your sister at dinner tonight. You two haven't said a word to each other all day, I'd gather."

"We said a few words." Mona glanced at her hands, remembering the tree and the ladder, and felt her shame. If only she had responded to her sister sooner. Mona had to climb down the tree without the help of the ladder, and in the process, had received a few cuts and scratches because of it. The memory made Mona even more irritated with Lisa. And that made her feel guilty.

"That might explain her tears, then." Her father twitched his fingers, a habit he often did while he talked. He ran his hand under his chin and sighed. "Mona, I tell you this story to remind you that your mother and I named you and Lisa after that portrait. One woman with two names. I know you and Lisa won't always see eye to eye, but you are *sisters*, united by love and blood—canvas and paint—brought into this world by the best Creator of all time, even better than DaVinci himself. You understand that, don't you?"

Mona gulped. She nodded and felt stinging in the corner of her eyes.

"This means that when fights and disagreements happen, you're expected to seek reconciliation. Not just you, but both of you. Or else you might ruin a good thing, the best thing there is. I would know…I spent years hating my brother, your uncle. He always seemed to get in my way, and those unresolved issues in our childhood soon became unresolved issues in our adulthood. Don't make those same mistakes I did, Mona. It's not worth it."

The tears were flowing freely now. Mona remembered the time when her Uncle Charlie came over after years of being away, the reunion bringing tears to everyone as her father hugged his brother. Mona and Lisa had been too young at the time to know what was going on, but Mona had understood that it was something important.

This was something important too. And it was as if her father's words were softening that hardened place within her chest, the place where she'd shut Lisa out for the past few days.

It wasn't Lisa's fault that her hair was shiny and smooth or that her feet were small. It wasn't her fault that she was extra social and good at making friends. It wasn't her fault that she was Mona's sister and looked up to her.

Mona regretted every hurtful thing she had ever done toward Lisa. She loved her sister very much; it was just hard to remember that all the time.

"Sweet Mona, why the tears?" Her father reached over and brushed the few drops of moisture off her cheeks.

"I just feel like I've ruined everything, Dad. First this tree and then all my lies. And now Pollie and Lisa! I feel like I've messed up too much and can't make things right." By now the tears were falling even harder, and Mona desperately needed to blow her nose.

Her father reached for the tissue box and passed it to Mona, reaching out to brush more stray tears in the process. "I know, sweetie, you're feeling the weight of it all, and rightly so. It's only right we should bear the burden of our mistakes, but we aren't supposed to bear them for long. There's such thing as forgiveness and grace, and I think it's about time you received some. It looks like you're ready to make things right, yes?"

"Yes, more than anything!" Mona blew her nose into the tissue, feeling the tightness in her chest loosen with every tear shed.

"Then receive it. Don't keep dragging around your guilt like a pack mule, forgetting what Jesus did on the cross. And take strides to make good choices. You won't always get it right, but it's how you react in times of trial or strain which really shows true character. Understood?"

She nodded. Mona wiped at her eyes and blew her nose one more time. She felt loads lighter and even felt compelled to action. "Do you think Lisa would mind if this prisoner left her cell for a few minutes?"

Her father cracked a smile, mirth in his eyes. "No, I don't think she'd mind that at all. In fact, I think she'd greatly accept it. As long as this prisoner is in bed before 9:00."

"Thanks, Dad!" Mona sat up and jumped in his arms.

Her father hugged her tight and placed a gentle kiss atop her head. "You know how much I love you?"

"How much?" Mona looked up into his eyes.

"More than all the art and history in the world, and way more than any of DaVinci's paintings are worth. And that's a whole, whole lot."

Chapter 11

Bear Good Fruit

The next morning, Mona checked on the tree before school. It stood tall, stretching its limbs toward the cloudless sky and swaying gently in the subtle breeze, its leaves rustling in greeting. It looked almost…friendly.

Something felt different.

Today's fruit was unlike any of the others. They were shaped like stars and the softest shade of pink she'd ever seen as if a peony had kissed the skin and made them blush. But it wasn't so much as what they looked like that rendered her intrigued as much as what she felt. For something *was* different. She was certain of it.

But what was it?

Not knowing why, Mona stretched her hand upward and

grasped one of the pale pink stars and twisted until it snapped from its stem. The subtlest aroma of something sweet reached her nose.

But it wasn't the sickening sweetness she'd smelt from the other fruits before this one—the kind of sweetness that masked the grossness that lay beneath. No, this sweetness was different. Almost pure.

Mona hesitated as she brought it closer to her mouth, sniffing it again with her nose. Should she do it? She remembered Pollie throwing up after eating the turquoise fruit and worried the same might happen to her. But for reasons she couldn't shake, Mona knew that wouldn't happen this time.

The pink skin brushed against her lips before she opened her mouth and took the littlest bite from the tip of the star.

The tangy sweetness exploded in her mouth, but with a gentleness she wasn't anticipating. It tasted…good. Really good. Mona stuffed the rest of the fruit in her mouth and sighed with delight. This was the best thing she'd ever tasted, but it was the feeling of hope which followed that ultimately warmed her stomach.

Mona felt that she could do anything, that perhaps choosing the right thing wasn't so hard after all. Maybe things would even turn out all right with Pollie.

* * *

Almost three weeks had gone by, and things still hadn't improved with their friendship. Pollie hardly acknowledged her at school, but Mona felt that she could handle the awkwardness since everything with Lisa had improved greatly. Her sister wasn't as annoying as she had thought; maybe Lisa was growing up, or maybe Mona was.

Not to mention, the fruit on the tree continued to change shape and color daily, improving in taste each time. Mona thought that she could handle another week or so being grounded if the tree continued to produce delicious fruit. It was making all the difference.

Mona was tackling her grounding period with a new perspective, and it made the time pass by quickly.

Almost too quickly.

Her Geography project was due at the end of the week, and Mona had hardly consulted her group about her progress. When the project was assigned, she had thought it would be a dream to work with Pollie, but now it was turning into a nightmare. It *was* a saving grace to have Jeremy as the third member of their group who was unknowingly playing the middle-man, communicating anything that needed communicating between the two of them. But even still, Mona wasn't sure how they'd pull off an A.

She had done all her research on Egypt and Scotland, and she was wrapping up her facts on New Zealand later tonight. She couldn't even remember what countries Pollie was researching, so she could only hope it would all work out. They eventually needed to come together to compare and contrast their facts.

Mona massaged her temples as she sat up in bed. If she didn't stop her racing thoughts, she was sure her head would scream. She threw off her covers and sat up, rubbing the crust out of her morning eyes.

She'd been sleeping well the past couple of nights, her dreams calm and laced with peaceful musings. She felt more confident about going to school, too, and the more she thought about it, the more she wondered if the tree had anything to do with it.

Mona pushed herself to a standing position and began to get ready for the day. Maybe today would be the turning point and Pollie would finally talk to her. They had to present their project on Friday, so it was bound to happen soon. Right?

Once downstairs, Mona grabbed a granola bar from the cabinet and plunked down at the kitchen island.

Lisa capered down the stairs soon after, a lightness in her step, obviously founded in the newness of a new day.

Mona laughed. Lisa was always the morning person.

"Mornin'!" Lisa skipped into the kitchen, grabbing a bowl from the cabinet and milk from the fridge. She then went to the pantry and grabbed a box of Captain Crunch before putting it all together: first the cereal and then the milk.

"Leese, slow down!" Mona tried to steady the bowl after Lisa unintentionally set it tottering in her haste to retrieve a spoon. "Your breakfast will end up on the floor at this rate."

"I'm being careful." Lisa giggled, spooning the crunchy flakes into her mouth.

"Sure, you are. You want some cereal with that milk?" Mona teased, laughing at the imbalanced quantities. *Who puts that much milk in their cereal?*

"Oh be quiet. I ate too much yesterday and don't have enough for this morning. The extra milk is my way of deception. If there isn't enough cereal in my bowl, at least I'll pretend there is." Lisa continued to heap her spoon, ignoring Mona's perplexed expression.

"You're something else, Leese."

The sisters laughed and continued to eat their breakfasts until their mother came downstairs. She looked pleased and quickly made a smoothie before ushering her children toward the garage.

"Wait, I forgot something!" Mona snatched up her

backpack and jogged out the back door and toward the hidden grove. Once there, she looked up at the tree which seemed to be even taller than it was yesterday, its fruit tiny clusters of what looked to be some sort of blackberries. The color was the deepest blue, rivaling the depth of the ocean, and Mona was sure it would taste just as sweet as all the rest.

Since the day of the pale pink stars, she'd been eating the tree's fruit without reservation. And today was no different. Mona grabbed hold of a cluster of deep blue berries and plucked them off the tree. She plopped a few into her mouth and felt the juice dribble down her chin.

They tasted like ice cream and sunshine. If courage and peace had flavors, she was sure it would be this, for she now felt as light as a feather and brave enough to handle anything. Mona grabbed a few more and stuffed them into the front pouch of her bag.

Ever since she'd had that "lying talk" with her parents, Mona had learned to be more honest. On the day of the pale pink stars, she had told her parents that she'd eaten the fruit and then had given them some to try for themselves.

She was sure her father must have been replaying the story of Adam and Eve in his head as she held out the fruit for him to taste. But it was a completely different situation, and she wasn't trying to tempt anybody. There was nothing wrong or off limits about the fruit this time. Instead, she felt that she was *supposed* to eat it.

Her father had hesitantly taken a bite along with her mother and sister, all of them leery about anything magical; but they had all agreed it was the best fruit any of them had ever tasted. And for some reason, after Mona told her parents what she'd done, the pale pink stars seemed to taste even better.

Her parents were still skeptical about the fruit changing daily, but they felt better knowing it was *good* rather than harmful. They chalked it up to the fact that "God provides miracles and sometimes things just can't be explained by mortal men—like a little kiss from Heaven."

Mona was all too grateful they hadn't called the tree black magic like Pollie's mother had.

Looking back at the tree now, it looked contented and pleased, like it was satisfied with its produce.

Mona placed her hand on the tree's trunk and smiled upward. "Thank you. I haven't always been kind to you, and I'm sorry for that. You *have* made things exceedingly complicated, you know. But I feel as if maybe you and I can finally be friends. Just keep behaving, please."

The tree ruffled its leaves and swayed in the breeze as if it was replying to her. A rustle on the wind rushed past her ear, whispering, *"Bear good fruit."*

"Who said that?" Mona turned, expecting to see someone step out of the forest, but she was alone. Only a few starlings twittered overhead.

Again, the telltale rustle of the wind in the leaves came once more, but this time with something added. *"Bear good fruit. Then passage is granted."* The voice was both soft and deep as if it was coming from beneath the earth.

Mona felt now that it must be the tree. But how? Really, she shouldn't be all that surprised considering the tree's history, but an audible voice was the last thing she had expected. And bear good fruit? That was the tree's job, not hers! What did the tree mean by it?

The last time she checked, she wasn't the one who had been planted or rooted in the ground. Maybe the tree was stranger than she had thought.

And what passage would be granted? To where? What on earth was this tree talking about?

"Mona!" her mother's voice echoed from somewhere within the house, and her tone seemed hurried.

Mona knew if she didn't leave the tree now, she'd be late for school. She quickly zipped up her bag and slung it over her shoulders before walking away.

As she left the path, she didn't miss the subtle whispers

still rustling in the distance. *"Bear good fruit. Then passage is granted."*

If only she understood what that meant.

Chapter 12

A New Friend

The day proceeded as it had since the start of the school year, the only noticeable difference being the fact that Mona was starting to enjoy it. No, things weren't perfect, and she still didn't have many friends—not to mention that Pollie was still ignoring her. But she was slowly becoming more accustomed to the daily routine and didn't mind her classes. Having schoolwork to distract her was something she was rather thankful for.

It was already lunchtime and as Mona was about to take a bite of her sandwich, someone fell into the seat next to her, bumping into the table and pushing it out from underneath Mona's elbows.

Losing her hold, Mona dropped her sandwich onto her

lap, some of it falling on the floor. "Are you kidding me?" she groaned as she peeled the contents of her sandwich off her jeans. A large mustard stain poked through beneath the lettuce.

Mona clenched her fists, irritation burning in her gut. Who had caused this? She looked up to see the sheepish face of Jeremy nervously smiling back at her.

"Was that my fault?" he asked, running a hand through his auburn curls. "My dad always said I moved too fast for my own good. Guess he was right." In his other hand, he held fast to a comic book. *Peter Pan?* Since when was that a comic?

"It sure was." Mona scowled, trying to dab at the stain with her napkin while picking the remains of her sandwich up off the floor. *What a waste.*

"Here, let me help." Jeremy placed his comic book on the table and reached into his lunch bag, pulling out a Tide-to-Go stick.

Mona paused enough to glare at him, her scowl easing into a quirked brow.

"What? If you think this is weird, you should see my brother, Derick. His backpack is like a portable laundromat; he uses dryer sheets like they're tissue boxes." He laughed and a large dimple formed in his left cheek, making him look rather charming. Mona found that she quite liked it and wished she had one of her own.

"Fair enough. I just think it's a little strange is all." Mona felt herself smile despite her irritation and grabbed the stick, dabbing lightly at her jeans. The mustard was surrendering to the power of the remover; she just had to suffer her jeans being a little wet until they dried. Better than the alternative.

Mona handed back the Tide-to-Go. "Thanks." She didn't know what else to say.

"Sorry about that, I shouldn't have sat down so hard." Jeremy pulled out his sandwich and offered Mona the other half. "Here, take it. It's the least I can do since I rendered yours utterly useless."

"I couldn't, thanks tho—"

"All right, suit yourself. Just remain ravenously hungry while I devour this superbly, delicious, hand-carved turkey and fresh provolone sandwich on wheat bread all by mys—"

"Fine. I'll take it." Mona gave in, clearly seeing how there was no point in arguing. Jeremy would be singing the sandwich's praises all day at this rate.

"Thought you might." He winked and took a bite of his half, humming a tune to himself.

Mona rolled her eyes and took a small bite, letting the flavor dance over her tongue; she sighed inwardly, trying to suppress a smile. *Is this smoked turkey?* Her favorite kind—

perhaps she should laude the sandwich too.

She glanced back at Jeremy; he had stopped humming and was looking at her expectantly. Mona's cheeks heated under his gaze. *Why is he watching me eat?* She needed to change the subject.

"So uh, why are you here?" Mona swallowed her bite and took another, waiting for his response.

"Oh, you know. My family seems to think I'd benefit from some civilized education. I don't see why, though." Jeremy took another bite of his sandwich and smiled with his mouth full, seeming to purposefully disprove his point.

Mona snorted, nearly choking on a piece of lettuce. "That's not what I meant." She recovered and finished her sentence. "I was asking why you're here, at this lunch table, with me…" She didn't want to sound like she didn't want him there, but he'd never sat with her before. Why now?

"Ah. The boys and I had an argument of sorts. Arm wrestling matches can get pretty heated, especially if there's cheating involved. So, I left to clear the air. Should be fine by tomorrow," Jeremy said like it was nothing.

Mona silently wished she could say the same about her and Pollie. How come boys could forgive so easily? Was it something they all agreed to beforehand, like a pact of sorts?

"Besides, I've noticed you sit alone most days. Figured

you could use a friend." Jeremy smiled so that his dimple showed once more. Mona found now that she was annoyed by it.

"I see." She wasn't sure if she was flattered or infuriated by Jeremy's words. She didn't want to be his charity case, for him to befriend her just out of pity. That would be worse than having no friends at all. She cast her gaze on the table, hurt and embarrassment roiling in her gut.

"Are you okay?" Jeremy asked, finishing his last bite.

"It doesn't matter, I should get going—" Mona stood, grabbed her backpack, and was about to sling it over her shoulder when Jeremy's hand reached for hers. Mona stilled instantly. Why on earth was he holding her hand? Wouldn't the whole cafeteria see? The thought made her stomach do weird things.

"Wait. Mona, hold on." Jeremy let go of her hand as Mona reclaimed her seat, her pulse returning to normal. "I told you about my older brother, Derick, but I also have a younger sister, Ariel. If she's ever bothered by something, she has this look on her face—the same one I saw on yours just now. I know I may be a little dense, but I honestly don't know what I've done."

Ariel? Was it the same as Lisa's friend? Most likely— how many other girls were named Ariel in this school? Plus, the little girl had red hair like her brother…

Mona couldn't figure Jeremy out. What kind of middle-schooler carried a Tide-to-Go stick and gave half of his sandwich to someone he hardly knew? What kind of boy read *Peter Pan* comics and had the perception of a hawk to know when something was wrong? Yes, Mona was deeply perplexed, but perhaps she was jumping to conclusions. Maybe Jeremy honestly wanted to be her friend.

"You've done nothing. I think I'm just homesick. And I miss having friends who genuinely want to be around me," Mona began. "I don't want your pity friendship no matter how willing you are to give it."

"And you shan't have it. I don't give half my sandwich to just anyone. Come on, Mona. Can't we be friends? We *are* Geography partners, after all."

Was he being serious? The more she scrutinized his sincerity, the more she felt there was nothing false in its place. He genuinely wanted to be her friend.

Mona stretched her hand forward, ready to make it a sure thing.

"What are you doing?" Jeremy eyed her hand suspiciously, a smirk tugging at the corner of his mouth.

"We must shake on it. That if we ever have a falling out of sorts, you'll promise to still be my friend and come back the next day, as you do with your boys. I can't take losing anyone else."

Jeremy reached out and grasped her hand, pumping their arms up and down like one would a water spigot. "You have my word." He let go and took a long swig from his water.

Mona found herself smiling, happy to have made a new friend. She grabbed her empty lunch bag and unzipped her backpack to stuff it inside, surprised at seeing the blackberries she had put there from earlier. In the chaos of lunch, she'd forgotten about the fruit!

Mona reached her hand into the pocket and withdrew a string of perfectly ripe berries. They smelt heavenly and looked even more delicious than she remembered.

"Woah! What are those?" Jeremy placed his bottle down and gaped. "I wouldn't have given you my sandwich if I knew you were holding out on me. You hustled me for food!" He laughed and reached toward the fruit, poking it with his finger.

"I honestly forgot about them until now." Mona's mouth watered at the sight of them, and before she knew it, she plucked a few off the remaining vine and gave some to Jeremy before he even had to ask. "Trust me, they are very good."

Mona watched as Jeremy shrugged his shoulders and leaned his head back, pouring the berries from his hand like a funnel into his mouth. Dark blue juice stained his fingertips and the corners of his lips as he chewed, clearly very satisfied.

"Those were so good! Where did you get them?" he asked, and this time, Mona was truthful about answering.

She told him about the tree.

Jeremy's eyes grew wide, taking everything in. His hand reached for his comic book as Mona continued to talk, the story of the tree and its fruit seeming to captivate his every fiber. When she finished, he opened up the comic and flipped through some pages, muttering to himself, "Interesting, very interesting." It seemed like he was searching for answers, but to what?

Mona laughed. She'd never understand boys, but at least Jeremy had found what she said *interesting.* That was a good place for their friendship to start.

For some reason, she had a feeling the tree would be proud to know its fruit was being shared—perhaps this is what it meant when it said, *"Bear good fruit."* Maybe all Mona had to do was share it with others…

But she *had* shared the fruit with Pollie—that had been the problem. Something must have changed to make it taste better, but Mona had no clue as to what that might be.

If only she had been truthful with Pollie from the beginning. Their group presentation was on Friday, and if they didn't reconcile before then, they were in for some serious failure—all three of them—including Jeremy who had nothing to do with what happened. Their bad grade wouldn't be fair to him, and Mona felt that she owed him a decent grade for the sake of their newfound friendship.

Mona needed to fix things, and she only had so much time.

Chapter 13

A Game Plan

"Focus, Jeremy! She'll be here any minute," Mona whispered.

It was a convenient miracle that the principal implemented a change to their schedule. All fifth and sixth-graders were to have a study hall in the library on Wednesdays and all seventh and eighth-graders were to have one on Thursdays. This was only the first week with this new schedule in place, but already Mona was treasuring it as one of her favorite blocks.

It gave her and Jeremy ample time to execute the plan they had come up with over the past few days. And today was the day! If it didn't work, she was sure tomorrow's presentation would cause her class and Mr. Frankweiler to cut the tension in the room with a proverbial knife.

Anything but that. Yes, this free block would be the surest way to victory. She was relying on Jeremy to make it happen.

Mona stood up and slung her bag over her shoulder. She made to move in the direction toward the stacks and rows of books, but before she left, she prodded Jeremy once more.

"Remember, you want to bring her to the section on 'World History'. Tell her you have a question about a book for our project and need her help. When she comes over, we'll corner her together." Mona's heart pounded like a million flapping blue jays, her stomach somersaulting at the thought. Could they pull this off? And would Pollie hate her even more after it all happened?

"I know, I know. Now go hide. We'll be over soon." Jeremy shooed her in the direction of the stacks and resumed his nonchalance, flipping through the pages of his comic book. Was he still reading that thing?

Mona silently prayed that this whole ordeal would work out. She crept stealthily to a back corner of the library, a quiet alcove where tall shelves of books on world history towered around her. There was a stool nearby in case one needed to peruse the upper shelves, but Mona stood on it for other purposes, parting a few books aside so she could peer through the bookcase. Perhaps she'd be able to glimpse Pollie coming in and Jeremy's success.

It was no use, there was another shelf blocking her view. She'd have to stand by, blinded with her nerves, awaiting the fate of all their friendships.

Mona's ears pricked up at the sound of familiar, hushed, voices. It was Jeremy, and he was asking Pollie to come toward his table. Mona couldn't see what Pollie was doing, but she hadn't heard Pollie say no.

Mona strained her ears to catch their words, but it was proving rather difficult now that two eighth-grade girls had come to the aisle next to hers and were giggling over something clearly not related to academics. Why did they have to be so close? Couldn't they discuss the cuteness of boys in the bathroom or something?

Mona counted the seconds, her heart threatening to plummet for fear that her plan was collapsing in on itself. What was taking them so long?

Then she heard Jeremy's voice over the giggles of the girls. He was coming with Pollie!

Mona squeezed herself into a nook, a small space where the bookshelf didn't quite meet the wall, and waited. This would either turn out wonderfully or having the entire school burn down might prove a more positive outcome. Mona sucked her bottom lip and steadied her breathing. Her friends had just come into view and were walking toward her.

"As I was saying, I figured we could divide and conquer looking for that book. Information on North Korea is like finding a needle in a haystack…" Jeremy whispered, running a hand through his hair. Mona gave him credit; he was playing the part rather well.

"And you think an old book is gonna have more information than the modern internet?" Pollie crossed her arms over her chest, lifting a brow.

"Just help me look, all right?" Jeremy moved around Pollie so he was blocking the exit out of the alcove as he began searching the shelves.

"Fine." Pollie shrugged off her backpack and approached the shelf closest to where Mona was hiding.

Mona felt her pulse pound in her chest, beat against her temples, and churn in her stomach. She had to leave her hiding spot sooner or later, and in doing so, she had a feeling she'd be giving Pollie a heart attack in the process. Surely one of the best ways to begin mending their friendship…What on earth was she thinking?

As if reading her thoughts, Jeremy began speaking again, but this time rather oddly like it was some sort of code. "Where are *you*? Come on, little book, why can't *you* come out of hiding already?"

Mona couldn't waste any more time. She silently prayed

once again and then held her breath as she emerged from the shadows. At first, Pollie didn't see her, but then Pollie suddenly turned, hand flying to her chest in surprise. Her mouth opened to scream, but before any sound came out, Jeremy had his hand over her mouth, muffling the cry.

Fury burned in Pollie's eyes at being betrayed, and Mona only had so much time to smooth things over. Maybe it'd be best to start with an apology.

"Pollie, I'm so sorry," Mona whispered. "I'm sorry for everything. I didn't want to scare you like this, but we needed to talk, and this was all I could come up with."

"Yeeouch! She bit me!" Jeremy nearly yelled; he dropped his hand and shook it out, rubbing the spot.

"Shhh! You'll get us all in trouble!" Mona whisper-shouted

Pollie turned to run, but Jeremy was quicker. He was at least a head taller than both girls, and he wasn't about to let anyone pass him.

"Pollie, please. Let me just talk for a minute," Mona pleaded, her hope wavering.

"I'm not supposed to talk to you, Mona." Pollie gave up her retreat and turned around, her arms crossed once more over her chest. She wouldn't meet her friend's gaze.

"Not supposed to or won't? Listen, Pollie, I know I treated

you horribly and broke your trust, but I was lying to myself the whole time as well. I thought I could hide the tree and the fruit from everyone; I even convinced myself I might pull it off. I didn't know what I was getting myself into, and when you threw up…"

"It's fine, Mona, I didn't die," Pollie whispered even quieter.

"I know, but I should have told you about the tree sooner. I was in too deep. That's the thing; once you start one lie, the next one comes even quicker. And before you know it, you're practically drowning in a sea of them. I couldn't see straight, there was no land in sight, so the only place I knew where to go was under."

Mona was tempted to feel shame anew at the memory, but the conversation she'd had with her father came to mind and pushed the guilt away. She'd been given grace for her mistakes weeks ago, and even if Pollie never forgave her, she was already forgiven where it truly mattered most. The shame was no longer hers to claim.

"I'm truly sorry, Pollie. I understand if you don't forgive me or never want to be my friend again. I don't deserve it anyway, but our project deserves a good grade, and so does Jeremy."

"I thank you for that," he nodded.

"You don't get it. I do forgive you, Mona. I did the night I left your house. It's my mother I'm worried about. She isn't the forgiving type." Pollie began scuffing her toe against the fraying carpet. "Since the fruit incident, she's been acting rather strangely. She cries at night, mentioning something about a ship and forbidden magic, but anytime I ask her about it, she doesn't want to talk…If she even finds out that I've talked to you again, she's threatened to transfer me to another school."

A ship and magic? Mona's mind traced back to the night of the strange, silver cloud. Did that have anything to do with what Mrs. Archibald was crying about at night? Was the cloud ship Mona had seen a few weeks ago the same thing Mrs. Archibald was referring to?

Mona had a hunch it might be, but she didn't have room to think on that further. She was too busy trying to process the last thing Pollie had said about transferring schools. How could her one error cause this much pain for someone she cared about? And another school? Pollie had just moved from Michigan, and now she might have to transfer again?

Mona had never read *Romeo and Juliet,* but she knew enough about the story to determine her and Pollie's friendship was becoming precariously similar to it. A forbidden friendship was sure to venture into the realm of more lies; was it worth it? Something inside Mona told her that it was, but how would they do it? She was sick of hiding from the truth.

Pollie continued, "Our project will go fine, I just haven't done a good job of communicating. My mother frightens me too much to ever cross her, so I've been a little cold because of it." Pollie lifted her head and finally met Mona's gaze. "I'm sorry too, Mona. Truly. Your lies were used to spare hurt whereas my coldness has been the cause of it."

"I don't think either of us deserves that much credit." Mona laughed. "Do you think we can be friends again?"

"Please say yes and get it over with." Jeremy groaned in mock agony. "I don't think I can take this any longer."

"I don't know, Mona. I want to say yes, but my mother will kill me. Or you. I don't know which is worse." Pollie shuddered.

"Then I'll just have to come over and smooth things over with her." Mona walked over to where her backpack rested on the ground and picked it up. "I'll have to show her she can trust me, and maybe she'll agree to us being friends again."

"Does this require my help at all?" Jeremy questioned.

"This plan is risky enough as it is. If I invited a boy to my house, my mother would surely lose her head." Pollie frowned.

"Then count me in!" Jeremy laughed.

Pollie rolled her eyes.

The three left the alcove coming up with another scheme, and this time, Mona's heart was much lighter. There was still work to do, but at least there was a thread of hope.

That had to count for something.

Chapter 14

A Bitter Taste in the Wind

The hope Mona had felt earlier was now replaced with doubt. What was she thinking? She was still grounded and had about a week left; there was no way her parents would let her go to Pollie's house tomorrow after school!

Maybe that was for the best. The thought of meeting Pollie's mother again sent a shiver down Mona's spine; she was unforgiving and terrifying—like Aurora's Maleficent or Cinderella's Lady Tremaine—and Mona had already glimpsed some of that when Mrs. Archibald had stood in her foyer.

But Mona had to sum up the courage and ask her parents for permission. Though she was sure Mrs. Archibald wouldn't fault her daughter for interacting with Mona over a group presentation, she had little hope for interactions beyond that. If she couldn't win Mrs. Archibald over, Pollie might have to transfer or Mona have to take an oath of silence to never speak to her again.

Their plan had to work, but it didn't seem like it would.

Mona sat in her room, but it didn't last long before she started pacing. Tomorrow was Friday, which meant that the project was in less than twenty-four hours. Everything was on track for them to get a good grade, but that still didn't solve everything.

Mona sat down hard on her bed, exasperated from thinking. She could hardly sit still, her mind racing despite her attempt to slow the thoughts.

She sat up again and tugged on a jacket. She was going to talk to the tree; for some reason, she felt as if it might hold some answers. After that, then she'd talk to her parents and seek their permission for Friday.

Mona sprinted down the stairs and headed toward the back door, a restlessness churning in her stomach. She was almost outside when her mother's voice carried to her from the kitchen.

"Where are you off to in such a hurry, Mona?"

Mona slowed enough to say, "I'm going to the tree! I'll be back soon," before she left the house and ran to the alcove.

She'd talk to her mother soon, just not yet.

The sun was still shining, but in an hour, it would be setting over the tree line. She had a few things to figure out before then, so she only hoped the light would hold out a little while longer.

Mona stepped through the dense copse and entered the alcove, her gaze scanning over the faerie houses which seemed to have grown taller since her last visit. Had some squirrels burrowed underneath them and pushed the ground up?

She cast her gaze on the majestic boughs of her magic tree and her breath caught in her throat. It looked healthy and thriving in the waning sunlight, almost like it was glistening silver like the seed.

Mona had taken care to prune it and spend time with it every day after school for the past three weeks, and it was clear that her attention was proving good for the tree, for it radiated happiness—a sweetness—which seemed to linger in the air. And it looked as if it was happy to see her.

Mona stepped closer and stopped once her hand pressed firmly against the bark. She tilted her head skyward and looked up into the spindly limbs extending from the trunk, a view which belonged to the world of faeries. It was magic itself, and today's fruit—a brilliant yellow with a striking orange stripe down its middle—only made the sight all the more ethereal.

How could she have ever hated this tree? It was beautiful.

She reached upward and plucked one of the fruits from a low-hanging bough and sank her teeth into its fragile skin. A tangy juice dribbled onto her chin and down her fingertips. No matter how many new fruits this tree produced or how many times she ate of them, their sweetness always took her breath away.

What had caused the change in its taste? It went from vomit-inducing to tasting like Heaven on earth. That was something Mona was still trying to discern. But there were other, more pressing things to discuss first.

She sighed deeply and finally let all the words pooling in her mind tumble out like marbles from a bag. "I need to patch up my friendship with Pollie, but the only way to do that is through her mother. But there are serious issues with this. Her mother is basically Cruella de Vil—minus the killing puppies for their pelts thing—and she's not easy to talk to. Jeremy and I have plans to go over Pollie's house tomorrow after school, but I'm still grounded…so I have a feeling that my parents won't let me."

Mona paused to catch her breath, her grip tightening on the half-eaten fruit.

"I have thought about not asking my parents…and just *accidentally* catching a ride with Jeremy's mom after school tomorrow…but I have a feeling that won't work. Another thought was I go over Pollie's tonight and just tell my parents it's for the project tomorrow…they'd believe that more than the first!"

Mona bit her lip, deep in thought as a steady breeze whipped by and sent the branches of her magic tree dancing wildly. The wind was fierce all of a sudden, and the once sweet-smelling alcove now turned into a bitter chill, a warning of something worse to come.

Mona tugged her jacket even closer to her neck and was about to take another bite from her fruit when she stifled a cry. The yellowed skin was turning black inside, a foul stench already weaseling its way out of its core.

She dropped the soured fruit and took a step back, eyeing the tree suspiciously and trying to steady her racing heart. The bark turned a darker shade, its trunk losing its silver sheen.

"What's going on?" Mona choaked out.

The wind shifted and pulled at her frizzy hair, some strands flying into her mouth. She tried pulling at them with her hand, the taste of bitter juice replacing the once-sweet kind still on her fingertips.

Mona couldn't help thinking that the tree was angry with

her. For some reason, she felt she had caused this…but how? She had only spoken aloud her thoughts, had been trying to gain wisdom or insight on what to do. And now? It seemed this alcove was trying to swallow her whole.

Had she said something wrong? And then a thought struck her. She *had* been pondering some things that weren't necessarily good or honest. Had that been her fear talking? She was pretty concerned about losing Pollie's friendship, but there was a perfectly viable solution right before her eyes…she just had to ask her parents. They might say no, but she wouldn't know until she tried.

How easy it was to forget the truth in the face of fear. She wouldn't lie or deceive to get her way, not this time.

As if reading her thoughts, the wind died down and stopped rattling the branches above her. The aroma of the alcove also seemed to return to its original sweetness, the bitter sting dissipating with the gale. The tree resumed its glimmer once more, its silver flecks dancing in and out of the sunlight. It was peaceful—the stillness that takes place after a storm.

Something on the ground caught Mona's attention. It was yellow and sweet and seemed to beckon her nearer as it gleamed in the remaining light; it was her half-eaten fruit.

Mona bent to pick it up and gasped when the yellowed

skin came clearer into focus. She stood up with the fruit in her hands, turning it over again and again to make sense of what she was seeing.

Hadn't this fruit just gone black and sour? Now it was the complete opposite—juicy and radiating sweetness. But it was different in a way. This time the sweetness of the fruit seemed to understand the consequences of what it had just been, its bruised and soured flesh now made like new. A sense of shame washed clean by some sort of forgiveness and grace.

A tear slipped down Mona's cheek, dripping from her nose and onto the ground by her feet. She couldn't help but feel that this yellow fruit was somehow a reflection of herself, that this tree, on a deeper level, was a reflection of her very being. How could this be?

Mona flinched, her stomach suddenly in knots when something brushed the tears from her cheek. She looked up to see the tree swaying and extending one of its branches in her direction as if it was trying to comfort her.

The tree's coming alive!

It had never done that before! She knew it could talk, but now it was moving freely, like a human stretching its limbs and waking from a slumber, though its roots remained firmly in place.

That thought eased Mona's temporal fears, for now—at

least the tree wasn't walking around like one of Tolkien's Ents. Those talking, walking trees were both incredible and scary; she didn't want to accidentally be stepped on by one of their thickly rooted feet.

The tree continued its stretching as a gentle breeze stirred in the alcove, caressing Mona's skin and kissing a whispered truth against her ear. It was the same voice as last time, deep and bellowing up from the earth—the voice from the tree itself.

"Every healthy plant bears good fruit, Mona. And likewise with you. Remember who you were created to be," the tree began, pausing before turning its voice into something more poetic.

"Bear good fruit

Upon this tree

And then passage granted

by such as me."

Mona pondered its words as if hearing a tree's voice dancing in the wind was normal. As if being comforted by one was normal too. The tree seemed to both understand *and* want to communicate with her.

She wasn't afraid of it, though; in fact, she was relieved.

For reasons she couldn't explain, she felt this tree was now her friend. That brought her list of new friends to three.

She didn't question it, for she knew that somehow the tree was connected to her. And she was slowly beginning to understand that perhaps it wasn't so much the tree's job of bearing good fruit as much as it was her own.

But what did the tree mean when it said *'then passage granted by such as me?'* What passage? How would a tree even do that? That was still something Mona didn't understand.

But then again, stranger things had already happened. She wouldn't put it past a talking tree to do something like grant passage to somewhere…but where?

Hopefully, she'd find out soon.

Chapter 15

Bending the Rules

Mona walked slowly back to the house, pausing before opening the door. She tilted her head skyward; it wasn't yet 5:00, but the stars were beginning to poke their heads out behind the clouds—the telltale sign of winter nights approaching.

Lord, give me strength, Mona silently prayed before entering inside, trying to steady her nerves. She found her mom sitting at the kitchen table, sifting through paperwork.

"What are those?" Mona questioned, her stomach fluttering like a butterfly's wings as she sat down across from her mother. Why was she still nervous to ask about Pollie's house? Hadn't she already made up her mind? Mona sighed— she had, but that still didn't change anything…

"I know you well enough, Mona, to guess you already know these are bills and that you're really trying to ask something else. Your sigh says it all." Her mother smiled knowingly; her brow quirked up in question. "Am I right?" She folded the bills and clipped them together before placing them back on the table and leaning closer to her daughter, ready to listen.

"Well, you're not wrong." Mona rubbed the back of her neck and suppressed an awkward smile, the weight of her question lying heavily on her shoulders.

"What is it? You know you can tell me anything, sweetie." Her mother reached over and grabbed Mona's hand, her smile, both gentle and serious, prodding Mona to continue.

"I know. It's just, there's been a lot on my mind and I don't even know how to start."

"How about at the beginning," her mother suggested.

"Okay." Mona took a deep breath. *Here goes nothing.* She began, "Do you remember all the lies I told about the fruit? Well, they ruined everything, especially the one friendship I cared about most. Pollie can't even speak to me without her mom threatening to move her to another school. Don't you find that a bit drastic?" Now that she'd begun speaking, Mona felt she couldn't stop. "It's been almost three weeks of this torture!"

"Oftentimes our actions have consequences, sweetie. And sometimes those consequences don't always seem fair," her mother said, her gaze watching Mona carefully. "Though I agree with you, it is a bit drastic. Everyone makes mistakes. There should always be room for forgiveness."

"But Pollie said she *did* forgive me, it's just her mother who hasn't. Pollie, Jeremy, and I have this group presentation tomorrow in Geo, so we *have to* talk during that, but once it's over, the only friend I'll have is Jeremy—Jeremy, mom! A boy who carries Tide-to-Go in his lunch box and reads a comic book like it's *his* best friend. It can't come to that." Mona placed both hands in her hair and bunched them in her curls, exasperation getting to her.

"Mona, breathe. And take your hands out of your hair. You're going to rip some out," her mother said gently.

Mona relaxed an inch and released an exasperated breath rather than her hands. "What am I going to do? Every idea I have seems hopeless."

"What are some of your ideas?"

"Well, the first two aren't any good, just ask the tree…" Mona paused.

"Ask the what?" Her mother's brow creased.

"But I had another idea, though I'm not sure you and Dad will agree to it." Mona bit her lip, fighting the blush creeping up her face. She always seemed to get nervous asking for something when chances were slim.

As if on cue, the garage door opened, muffled beyond the dining room wall, and was followed by the sound of a car's engine drawing nearer. Mona's father was home.

The car door shut and the garage door closing once more indicated that her dad would be coming in at any moment.

"How convenient. Why don't you wait with your question so you can also ask your father."

"Ask me what?" Her dad stepped in through the door, a large smile on his face. He placed his briefcase on the bench and hung his coat up on the rack before walking over to the table.

"Honey, you're home just in time. Mona has a question to ask us that she isn't sure if we'll agree to." Mona's mother quickly briefed her husband on the recent conversation while he nodded in all the right places.

Mona just watched, the anticipation building.

"All right, Mona, what do you have in mind?" her father questioned.

Mona gulped and began. She had waited long enough, and who knew, maybe her parents would understand. "I wanted to know if I could go over Pollie's house tomorrow after school and talk to her mother. I was thinking it might be the only way for me to mend what I've broken." Mona wiped her clammy hands on her pants; the worst was over. She had finally done it.

Her mother and father shared a look, the kind that speaks volumes without the need for words. Mona wondered if she'd ever be able to do that with someone—to just know what they're thinking.

As if reading Mona's thoughts, both her parents cleared their throats, but it was her mother who began speaking first. "Mona, that's a very grown-up thing to do, and we're very proud of you for coming to that decision by yourself..."

"But...?" Mona could tell there must be a catch. There had to be.

"You're still grounded. You have about a week left, and rules are rules," her father finished. He had that same look in his eyes which showed that the decision was causing him pain as well.

Mona's heart sank. She knew it was too good to be true. Sure, she probably shouldn't have worried so much; it never hurt to ask. But it sure hurt to get rejected in the asking, especially when a friendship was at stake.

"Listen, Mona, your mother and I can tell that you've taken your punishment well, showing ownership with that tree and telling the truth. That doesn't go unnoticed. But I can't, in good conscience, let you go on Friday. However, since the month ends on Wednesday next week, why don't we plan for then? I think that's a reasonable enough solution."

Mona swallowed hard. She wouldn't be able to talk to Pollie for about five days, but it was better than a full week. She should count her blessings…that's if everything went right with Mrs. Archibald in the first place.

"So, on Wednesday I can go to Pollie's house?" Mona questioned. She was sure her eagerness soared through the roof.

"Yes." Her father smiled.

"And I'll go with you. A mother's touch is usually helpful in these types of situations." Her mother winked and reached once more for Mona's hands which were blessedly free and no longer tangled in her hair. "We really are proud of you, Mona. You're growing up." Her mother's eyes glistened with unshed tears.

The words warmed Mona's core. Sure, the answer hadn't been what she'd hoped for, but it was better than getting into more trouble for doing the wrong thing. Perhaps she really was growing up; but is this what it felt like? To make the right decisions when everything in her often wanted to fight for the wrong?

She didn't know, but she could only guess.

"Okay, I can wait." When Mona said it, she felt difficulty in accepting the truth. But it would have to do.

In the meantime, at least she had Jeremy. He was better than not having any friends at all. Besides, he wasn't all that bad.

In fact, she found him rather amusing when he wasn't so obnoxious.

A Presentation of Friends

Mona sat in Geography, her leg bouncing against her hand and her project on the desk before her. In a few minutes, it would be their group's turn to finally present to the class, but for some reason, Egypt, Scotland, and New Zealand didn't seem nearly as interesting now that she had to talk about them to people who probably didn't even care.

She again wished for the ground to swallow her whole. Yes, she'd have two friends by her side, but one of them couldn't talk to her and the other seemed to live on a planet of his own. For all intents and purposes, this project didn't look promising, and yet, their group was determined. Some way or another, they were going to pull it off. They had to. *Right?*

Perhaps after a few presentations, their group would

follow suit and blend in. Nothing could be worse than being the first to go.

Mr. Frankweiler cleared his throat, "Now, class, we will begin with our presentations in only a moment. Do I have a group who'd like to volunteer to start us off?"

Mona caught movement in her peripherals and turned to see Jeremy's hand waving in the air. No one else had raised their hands…it was just Jeremy, his hand waving like a white flag signaling surrender and defeat.

Mona sighed, her pulse picking up speed. *So much for not going first.* Leave it to Jeremy to volunteer the group. He seemed to have a penchant for waving his arm around.

"Great, thanks for volunteering, Mr. Panberly. The three of you, please step forward and get your things ready," Mr. Frankweiler said as he walked toward his desk at the front corner of the room. He leaned against the table and pushed his glasses further up his nose before crossing his arms over his chest, waiting.

Mona begrudgingly stood, gathering her things and making her way to the front of the room.

Pollie followed close behind, pinning up a poster of Nepal once she got to the board.

Their group had decided early on that Pollie would present first out of the three of them; the thought eased the nerves in Mona's stomach if only a little.

Why did Jeremy have to raise his hand? Mona looked over at him, trying her best to let him see her scowl; she wanted him to know just how much she appreciated it.

"What?" he whispered, quirking his brow while setting up his project.

"You know very well, *what*," Mona whispered back, placing her project on the table next to his, trying not to let her nerves show through her movements.

When she glanced up at Jeremy, there was that telltale smirk on his face, the one where his irksome dimple makes him appear sincere.

She hated him all the more for it.

Jeremy stepped closer, lowering his voice so only she could hear. "Don't be mad, Mona, it'll be over before you know it."

She sighed. He *was* right. The sooner they presented, the sooner they could all sit down and get on with the day. But the thought was bittersweet; the sooner this project was over, the longer the gap between now and Wednesday.

Mona had already gone weeks without talking to Pollie, but now knowing the reason *why* made the waiting even more torturous.

Torturous—what an appropriate word. Why was the

seventh grade such a torturous year? Mona's emotions had been through enough rollercoasters and stress this past month than they'd had the past almost thirteen years of her life.

Hopefully, a chat with Pollie's mother would bring promises of better things to come. The tree seemed to hint that bearing good fruit would help with that…and Mona was trying her best, even if she wasn't certain what that entailed.

Pollie cleared her throat, waking Mona from her thoughts. She glanced over at her friend who stood poised and ready to begin speaking; Pollie looked calm standing in front of everyone—something that Mona would never feel without her friends beside her.

Yes, they were a strange, random group, but they *were* friends—good ones at that. Pollie was all confidence and strength while Jeremy was all humor and insight. And Mona couldn't help but wonder if they saw good things in her, too. What did she have to offer their friendship?

"Good morning, everyone. Today I will be talking about Nepal, Iceland, and England. Let's start with Nepal since I put that picture up first," Pollie began.

Mona watched as her friend introduced the country, speaking eloquently and clearly; she resembled Wendy Darling, her brown tresses pulled back with a blue bow and confidence exuding in every word like she was telling a story to the lost boys.

Mona then glanced at Jeremy who stood beside her, his auburn curls toppling over his forehead and his freckles dotting the bridge of his nose. He looked like Peter Pan himself.

Odd how she never noticed the resemblance before. How did she fit into this group? Was she Tinkerbell? There was no way—she possessed no magic. With her curly hair, she was more of a Captain Hook—the villain…the deceiver.

Is that how Mrs. Archibald would always see her as? What about her friends? The thought felt like a weight in Mona's gut.

She closed her eyes and breathed deeply, trying to steady her racing thoughts once more. She had already received forgiveness and grace—she wasn't the same girl she was three weeks ago. She had changed. Now if only Mrs. Archibald could see that too.

"Cows are a sacred animal in Nepal, and because of this, Nepalis don't consume beef. They actually use their dung for cleansing purposes since it's considered pure," Pollie said, trying not to giggle.

There was a collective "Eww," amongst the class with a sporadic "That's so cool!" thrown in.

Pollie went on to talk about her other two countries and

once she finished, began clearing away her project to make room for Mona's.

"Great job," Mona whispered to Pollie as she scooted to the front of the room, beginning to set everything up.

"Thanks!" Pollie whispered back. "Even though I'm not supposed to talk to you, I'm here, cheering you on. You can do this, Mona."

Mona didn't feel ready, but with Pollie's encouragement, she felt newfound strength. Maybe she was worrying for no reason, but she couldn't think about that anymore; it was now or never.

She hung up her poster of New Zealand and cleared her throat before speaking. "I'm going to begin with the lonely island off the coast of Australia—New Zealand." Mona swallowed the lump in her throat and continued, "Similar to Pollie, I'll start with a fun fact. Filled with countless national parks and places to hike and kayak, New Zealand is also home to Hobbiton which plays a crucial role in the set of *The Lord of the Rings.*"

There was a roar of applause from the back corner of the room where two boys shouted in excitement.

"It appears we have some Tolkien fans in here," Mr. Frankweiler said, chuckling. "Please continue, Mona."

Mona smiled, her fears dissipating with the excitement of

the classroom. Maybe presenting didn't have to be so bad after all.

When she finally finished her three countries, she breathed a little easier.

Shortly after, Jeremy took center stage and stole the show. He presented his three countries with exuberance and thrill, sharing facts that intersected with those of Pollie and Mona's; even his limited information on North Korea was a huge hit.

Mona and Pollie exchanged glances, suppressing the need to laugh. Jeremy was a performer, through and through.

It looked like they were going to receive an A on their presentation, after all.

Now, all Mona had to do was wait until Wednesday.

Chapter 17

The Days Before

Mona was in her backyard, walking barefoot for what she felt would be one of the last times until spring. For the past couple of nights, the weather had been cooling down significantly, which was usually an indicator that her birthday was just around the corner.

She'd be turning thirteen in only a few days; she only hoped that things with Pollie would be smoothed out by then.

Mona stopped walking and glanced up at the waning sun, its light filtering through the canopy of trees around her. Instantly, she was taken back to the night she found the seed…the seed that would grow into a strange, fruit-bearing tree. She had wished for a beanstalk or to find a fairytale realm, but instead, she had gotten an extra conscience in its place. For some reason, this tree was connected with her—by some strand of magic—and it seemed to respond to her actions.

Maybe she was Tinkerbell, after all.

Mona laughed and continued her stroll, only stopping when she heard her name being called.

"Mona! Wait up!"

Mona turned to find Lisa running out of the house, a baggy sweatshirt encapsulating her limbs while unlaced shoes graced her feet.

"What are you doing in such a hurry, Leese?" Mona couldn't help but laugh.

"I saw you from my bedroom window and got curious. Are you going to see that tree again?" Lisa asked, her eyes wide.

"As a matter of fact, I am. Would you like to come?" Mona felt that having her sister along could be fun.

"Yes! I've been waiting to see it!" Lisa blurted, excitement fueling her steps.

"Waiting? Haven't you already been?" Mona already knew the answer. Lisa *had* seen the tree.

Lisa seemed to grow embarrassed by Mona's question as evidence by the lowering of her head and her whispered response. "Well, I may have seen it a little...I went the night

I found the fruit and…that time with the ladder…" Lisa frowned. "I felt bad so I haven't been back since…"

Yes, Mona remembered that night. How everything had crashed around her feet and how she'd lost her only friend because of it. Time and forgiveness certainly changed things.

"But I've been taking care of the tree for the past weeks, why haven't you come then?"

"Because any time I asked mom, she said it was something you had to do alone. 'Her punishment can't be turned into a fun game,' she'd say. But it's now Tuesday and tomorrow you're off the hook, right?"

"Yes," *and it can't come soon enough,* Mona whispered under her breath. The weekend and past two days at school had been excruciatingly painful. She and Pollie hadn't spoken a word since their presentation, only exchanging occasional glances in class.

Though he wouldn't say as much, Mona could tell that Jeremy was getting tired of being their middleman again. She couldn't blame him; she was tired of it too.

Lisa followed close behind Mona as the two sisters stepped into the tucked-away alcove. A gasp sounded behind Mona, and when she turned around, Lisa's hand was covering her mouth, her eyes wider than before.

Mona laughed and turned to face the grove; it *was* a

magical sight. The faerie houses were taller than her head now. Something else must be making them grow besides the squirrels; they only had so much power when it came to burrowing.

The tree swayed in welcome, rustling its leaves and glistening with a silvery sheen as if winking at them. It looked to have grown even taller than yesterday, and a sweet aroma circulated about the small enclosure, kissing Mona's skin as the wind tugged on her hair.

"It didn't look like this the last time I saw it." Lisa marveled, her eyes roving over the glistening timber and surrounding houses.

"I can say the same thing." Mona shared in the awe, wondering just how tall everything had grown.

As if in response, one of the tree's branches extended toward her, a pink berry at its tip.

Lisa's eyes widened in shock, her mouth open like a trout.

"Don't be afraid, Leese. The tree's been doing that for a few days now—as if it's just stretching its limbs and coming to life. It won't hurt you." Mona smiled.

"Di-did it scare *you?* The first time it happened, I mean..." Lisa questioned, hesitantly extending her hand to grab the tree's offering.

"Yeah, it definitely shocked me! If I'd been in the tree at

the time, I probably would have fallen out!" Mona laughed and looked at the limbs above her. "I think the tree was only trying to comfort me or help me; it seems to like that sort of thing. I'm just thankful it hadn't tried to 'help' me while I was pruning it."

Lisa nodded, still staring at the swaying tree with uncertainty in her eyes. And then she moved her gaze to the fruit in her hand, unsure of what to do with it.

"Don't worry, Leese. I've told Mom and Dad about how the tree moves now and they aren't concerned. Well, maybe they're more in denial. They just think it's because of the wind." Mona was suddenly grateful to be known for her wild imagination; it made situations like this less dramatic. If Mona had been a quiet child who was serious and lacked imagination, then she was sure her parents would be more worried.

"It's perfectly safe to eat. It's like the other ones I've given you, remember? Here, I'll show you." Mona stretched her arm upward to grab one of the berries when a tree branch lowered to her level and offered her one instead. "Thank you." Mona patted its trunk.

She took the berry and placed it on her tongue, savoring the taste of the sweet skin before sinking her teeth into it. Today's fruit was as tart as a raspberry and as sweet as a watermelon, a fresh flavor that danced on the tastebuds.

Seeing her sister eat the fruit, Lisa took a bite and smiled. "It tastes just as good as the others! I don't know why the tree makes it seem so scary. Maybe it's because I...I don't know..." she grew quiet, her eyes on the ground.

Mona could tell that Lisa still felt bad about that night. Things had grown so much better between them since then, but even still, they hadn't really had the chance to hang out much with Mona being grounded and all her endless hours of homework.

Mona forgot that being a little sister sometimes brings insecurity; her mother had warned her as much.

Before their move to New England, the two sisters had gotten into an argument over something silly. It hadn't been a big deal, but it was enough for their mother to take Mona aside and talk with her. Seated in their backyard underneath the painted desert sky, shades of reds and oranges dancing above them, the beautiful scenery was the perfect backdrop for a reprimand.

"Remember, Mona. Don't be too eager to grow up that you forget about your sister. She looks up to you more than you know," her mother paused. "Sometimes being a little sister brings insecurity, and when you choose to spend time with her, I can guarantee, it will mean the world. Don't take that power for granted. Being an older sister is a gift few are given."

The words came back afresh, wafting over Mona as she stared at her sister. Mona had never been eager to grow up, but she was often eager to garner her independence and leave Lisa out of the loop. Over the past few weeks, she'd been learning to change that. Her mother had been right.

"It's not your fault." Mona felt the need to reassure her sister.

Lisa picked her head up, listening.

"I was mad at you at the time, but I think I was madder at myself if anything." Mona paused and swallowed, feeling the truth tumble out. "I lied to you the morning of the first day of school. I wasn't scared—I was terrified, but I didn't know how to show it. Growing up is hard sometimes." Mona sighed, a weight lifting from her shoulders that she didn't know was there. "You're a great sis, Leese. I think I admire you more than I even know," she said softly, the truth borderline embarrassing to admit.

Before Mona knew it, Lisa was in her arms, crying. In fact, both girls were crying, their silent tears a song of healing and understanding. And then the tears turned into laughter.

"I love you, Mona," Lisa said, her round eyes staring up at her sister.

"I love you too," Mona replied, her heart full as she hugged Lisa tighter.

Perhaps they really were like the Mona Lisa after all; a real-life painting of two sisters sharing a name—a bond of canvas and paint, of love and blood.

Chapter 18

Anticipation

"Are you gonna finish that? Mona?" Jeremy prodded, poking her on the shoulder. "Hello, anybody home?"

"What? Can't you see I'm thinking?" Mona brushed his hand away, ignoring him and her half-eaten sandwich on the table before her.

"Well, can't you think while I eat your castaways?"

"Sure, why not." Mona shrugged and leaned her chin on her upturned hand, thinking once again as the chaos of the lunchroom swirled around her.

"Thanks!" Jeremy grabbed her sandwich and dug in, his mouth chewing happily in unison to Mona's thoughts.

Since that first day Jeremy had joined her at the lunch table, he had decided to stay, enjoying Mona's company and their schemes over the stupidity of his friends'. Though Jeremy remained forever loyal to them, as such as their friendship required.

Mona found she didn't mind. She liked having Jeremy around; he was entertaining and proving to be a solid friend. But there were more pressing things on her mind.

Today's the day. Mona would be going over to Pollie's house later to see if she could win over her mother. The task seemed daunting, even more so knowing that she probably wouldn't be welcomed. Nothing like smoothing things over by just showing up unexpectedly.

But what other choice did she have? She'd be rejected before even having the chance to say a word.

"What time should I be over at your house again?" Jeremy asked with his mouth full.

Oh yes, and Jeremy would be going to Pollie's too. Truly, the more Mona thought over the plans, the more this all seemed hopeless.

Pollie had mentioned that her mother would lose it if a boy showed up at her house. Well, here was double the reason for her mother to flip all the more.

Mona cast a sideways glance at Jeremy, who was now taking a long swig of water from his water bottle.

"Your parents can drop you off around 6:00. We'll be

heading to Pollie's shortly after. She gave you her address, right?" Mona questioned, her palms suddenly growing clammy.

Jeremy's eyes grew wide as he felt around in his pockets.

"Don't tell me you lost it." Mona groaned.

"Here it is!" Jeremy smirked, his dimple doing its obnoxious thing once again, proving he'd known where it was all along.

"I'll take tha—" Mona reached for the paper.

Jeremy snatched his hand out of her reach. "Nope! I'm holding onto it for keeps. You'll get it once I make it over to your house tonight." Jeremy stuffed the remaining sandwich into his mouth and grinned.

"You're impossible!" Mona rolled her eyes.

"So I've been told." Jeremy chewed and swallowed, grabbing another drink of water while Mona divulged once more into her thoughts.

Pollie would be expecting them close to 6:15, just after their family finished eating dinner.

It was currently 11:45; only about seven more hours until the dreaded meeting. The length of time between now and 6:15 felt like a chasm of darkness, ready to suck any life and hope down with it.

Was she being too dramatic? No, her friendship was at

stake, and she couldn't very well just have Jeremy as her only friend…Maybe Gretchen from Geography would be a viable option if things with Pollie never worked out. Oh, and she still had the tree…

"You're worrying again," Jeremy said, pulling Mona from her thoughts.

"Huh?" She pretended she didn't hear him.

"You're bouncing your leg like you've got a bazillion ants in your pants, and you keep twisting your hands together like this." Jeremy mimicked her actions, causing a small tug to pull up at the corner of Mona's mouth.

How on earth had he noticed that? Again, she was perplexed by Jeremy; nothing seemed to escape his surveillance.

"Just thinking about tonight," Mona said, feeling slightly better having vocalized her fear.

"Life's too short for that."

"Now you sound like my mother." Mona laughed.

"It's what mine always used to say." Jeremy shrugged, his smile turning into something more somber.

Used to? But that would imply…Mona didn't miss the way Jeremy's demeanor shifted. What had happened to his mother?

"Anyway, it will be fine. And if not, hey at least you still got me, right?" Jeremy joked, his smirk returning.

Mona's laugh was halfhearted; her heart was feeling too many things: fear for the loss of a friendship with Pollie and concern for Jeremy and his family.

There was even more to him than she'd thought. And if things with Pollie didn't work out, she'd have more than enough time to figure him out.

Still, what she wouldn't give to have them both.

* * *

Mona paced the length of her driveway, waiting for the telltale sign of a car's engine to come closer. She kept glancing at her watch; the time was only 5:58, but Jeremy should be there any minute.

She tugged the bag she was carrying closer to her body so the straps wouldn't keep falling off her shoulder. Hopefully, she wouldn't have to use what was inside, but it was better to be prepared. Maybe it would be just the magic she needed to make this night count.

"Mona, are you wearing shoes?" her mother hollered from the garage, breaking through her thoughts.

"Yes!" she shouted back. Unlike yesterday, Mona had put some on tonight. One should never venture out in public without a good pair of shoes; she'd learned that the hard way.

Once when her family decided to dine out, she'd left her shoes at home. Her father had to run into a nearby CVS and get a cheap pair of flip-flops for her to wear so they could finally go inside the restaurant.

Since then, her mother often felt the need to remind her to wear shoes. But for an occasion such as visiting Pollie's mother, one simply didn't forget to wear shoes. It would be like asking a shoe shiner to forget his polish—it just wasn't wise, like welcoming a death sentence.

Mona looked back down at her watch and it read 6:02. Jeremy was running late, and she didn't even have Pollie's address to leave without him.

"Gahh," Mona tugged on her hair as a car's engine sounded at the top of the driveway. It got closer and revealed headlights, followed by the car itself.

Jeremy was in the front seat, waving a piece of paper out the window like a banner in the wind. "Better late than never, right?"

The van pulled to a complete stop and Mona snatched the paper from his hand. It was Pollie's address.

"You could say that again," Mona joked, a sense of urgency in her words. She wanted to leave now or else they might be late. But first, she should probably greet Jeremy's driver. "Hi, I'm Mona, are you Jeremy's father?"

"Hi, Mona, I am. It's nice to meet you! Jeremy's told me a lot about you," he said warmly. He had similar hair to his son, except his was a darker auburn with tints of gray at the roots. Countless freckles speckled his cheeks like he had seen much of the sun. His face was both gentle and weathered, indicating age and lines of grief, though there was still a glimmer of youth trying to shine through. Mona couldn't help but think about Jeremy's mother.

"It's nice to meet you too, Mr. Panberly." Mona smiled, hoping to bring him some mirth.

"Hello, Peter, nice to see you again." Mona's mother had come up behind her and was now peeking into the car.

"Hi, Ellen, nice to see you too. I hope my kids behave tonight. What time should I pick them up by?" Mr. Panberly asked.

Kids? Were Jeremy's siblings coming too?

"I'm thinking this won't last more than an hour or so, so let's try a little after 7:00. Is Ariel still in the car? I know Lisa's been very excited to spend time with her tonight."

"I'm here!" Ariel opened the side door and stepped out, a canvas bag strung over her shoulder. She smiled brightly up at Mona's mother. "Can I see Lisa now?"

Mona *had* guessed correctly; this was the same Ariel as

before. She looked just like Jeremy the more she thought about it.

"Sure thing, sweetie," her mother said.

"Bye, Dad!" Ariel ran into the house.

"Ted's inside and will be watching the girls while I take these two to the Archibald's. Thank you for letting Jeremy join us; I know his support means a lot to Mona," her mother said.

"Of course, well, I hope all goes well—Pollie must know how blessed she is to have friends like you two." Mr. Panberly directed the last part to both Mona and Jeremy.

"Thank you, sir," Mona said, feeling the fear in her middle subside.

She only hoped that Pollie's mother would feel the same way.

Chapter 19

Mrs. Archibald

The drive to Pollie's house felt much longer than ten minutes, the retreating sun making room for a hazy night sky to fade into a murky twilight.

Mona glanced behind her and saw Jeremy's silhouette in the back seat, his eyes glinting in what little light remained. "You ready for this?" she asked.

"Are *you?* You've been staring back here for the entire ride," Jeremy jested.

"Not true! Mom, have I?" Mona questioned, her nerves getting the better of her.

"I think you're just nervous, Mona. It's going to be okay," her mother assured her. "We're almost there, and then it will be over before you know it."

True to her word, their car slowed and pulled into a driveway that led to a copper-colored house set on a small hill. It looked welcoming, and Mona couldn't help but feel the irony of the situation. Would the inside be as inviting as the house appeared on the outside?

The car stopped once it got to the top of the driveway, and Jeremy exited as soon as the engine shut off.

Mona sat in her seat, breathing deeply. She could feel her mother's eyes on her profile, watching her.

"Do you want to talk?" she asked.

Mona swallowed around the knot in her throat and tried to steady her breathing. "What if this doesn't work, Mom?"

"Then at least you can walk away knowing you tried. A mother bear will always protect her cubs; maybe the mother bear in that house has calmed down enough to listen to you."

Mona sighed. "I guess you're right. You're waiting in the car, right?"

"You kidding? *This* mother bear needs to protect *her* cub. I'll be beside you the entire time!"

"Thanks, Mom." Mona felt the pressure in her chest release. She wasn't doing this alone; that's why her mom and Jeremy had come with her. The thought strengthened her resolve.

They got out of the car and met Jeremy, who was patiently

waiting. He was glancing at the night sky as if in thought, his gaze far off and distant.

Mona looked up into the starry heavens, trying to see what he was looking at. Something bright seemed to wink in the sky, shining brightly only to fade once again. *What was that? A shooting star?* For some reason, the sight brought back memories of the silver, clouded ship she'd spotted a month ago.

Mona glanced back at Jeremy and wondered what he must be thinking; something in his eyes indicated longing for things forgotten.

Without so much as speaking any words, he stopped staring and joined Mona and her mother, walking nonchalantly with his hands behind his back.

If Mona wasn't so anxious, she would have liked to analyze Jeremy more and ask him what he was thinking. He was a conundrum, and he kept perplexing her.

The three of them continued their walk to the front door. The lights were on, shining through the inky darkness. The air smelt of Italian spices and herbs, and Mona wondered if that was the remnants of dinner wafting through the open window. She breathed deeply and said a silent prayer before opening the storm door and knocking on the wooden one underneath.

A few seconds went by before footsteps could be heard

approaching the door from the inside. A few more seconds and the lock clicked and the door opened, revealing an over-eager Pollie on the other side.

"Good, you're here! I thought you might have changed your mind!" Pollie reached out and practically dragged Mona into the house, Jeremy and Mona's mother following after them.

"Pollie, who's at the front door?" A distant voice sounded down the hallway.

Mona observed the interior of the home. It was very clean and ornately furnished like it belonged in some magazine. The floors were wide cedar planks and the two columns outlining an archway to the living room were made of thick timber. A picture of a large ship was displayed over the fireplace, and when Mona shifted to look down the hallway, she noted a crystal chandelier hanging over a dining table. If Mona wasn't mistaken, the décor seemed to belong to that of a captain's cabin on a ship. Was that intentional?

Perhaps this isn't a good idea.

"Pollie?" the voice drew closer and revealed the object of Mona's visit. Mrs. Archibald walked forward, her hair slicked back in a high ponytail, her stilettos echoing on the wooden floors.

When her gaze landed on Mona, a deep crease formed in

the line of her brow. She pursed her lips and crossed her arms, her legs spread apart as she leaned heavily on her right leg. "What are you doing here?" Her eyes continued to observe the company, and when they alighted on Jeremy, her scowl turned into shock.

Yes, this isn't a good idea at all.

"Hi, Mrs. Archibald. I-I wanted to come by and talk t-to you," Mona fumbled with her words, the taste of them seeming foreign on her tongue. How was she supposed to talk to this woman?

"What is there anything *you* could possibly say to me?" She glared.

Mona's mother stepped forward with her hands on her hips. "Please, Wendy, she's just a child. There's no need to be so crass."

This seemed to take Mrs. Archibald back a step as her face went from anger to irritation. "Fine, please proceed." She waved her hand like she was swatting away an annoying fly.

Mona cleared her throat and stepped forward. "I wanted to apologize, Mrs. Archibald. For lying to Pollie and giving her fruit that I knew nothing about. It was that mysterious seed which caused all of this."

"Mysterious seeds should be left well enough alone. It does no good believing in the make-believe, of lands far away," Mrs. Archibald growled.

Mona's palms grew clammy, words of defense on her tongue. "But what of imagination? Have you never dreamt of other worlds, Mrs. Archibald?"

"I have and that's the problem. At some point, you must learn to grow up. I don't want my dear Pollie to be friends with those who encourage foolish dreams, no matter how much one *longs* for them." Mrs. Archibald's scowl fell deeper, but it didn't look believable. "Before you know it, you'll get snatched away in the limbs of some tree and find it hard to ever get back…*to ever want to get back…*"

The more Mona looked at Mrs. Archibald, the more she felt that she was missing something. Why would Mrs. Archibald speak so vehemently against their imagination? They were kids, after all! And what was she saying about trees? How could the limbs snatch someone away? Where would it take them?

No, this kind of disdain seemed to come from something else, like a seed of bitterness growing roots. Mona could relate to some degree; the same had almost happened to her. But Mrs. Archibald seemed deeply troubled. What had caused it?

If a life without imagination was like a life without water, then Mrs. Archibald was more than dehydrated if that was the case.

"Mrs. Archibald, all I ask is that you let Pollie and I be friends again. I promise I won't do anything foolish like feed her poisonous berries. I won't make that mistake again," Mona pleaded.

"Mistakes are often made more than once. I would know. There's no joy in finding your dream only to have it taken from you and crushed at your feet."

Since when had they started talking about dreams? Mrs. Archibald was missing the point Mona was trying to make. She felt a hand on her shoulder and was surprised to see it was Jeremy's rather than her mother's.

He stepped forward, bowing slightly. "Mrs. Archibald, we've never met, but I wanted to say what a lovely home you have."

Mona rolled her eyes. Why was he doing this now?

Mrs. Archibald narrowed her eyes, scrutinizing him from head to toe. Mona didn't miss the way her eyes seemed to move from disbelief to skepticism to shock. "You look familiar," she muttered.

Jeremy looked unphased, almost as if he expected her to say that. "My father's name is Peter. Peter *Pan*berly, if that rings a bell."

Had the emphasis on his last name been intentional? Mona didn't doubt it. Jeremy was full of mysteries.

"Panberly," she whispered the name in reverence as her hand reached toward her lips. *"Peter...?"* A gentle smile pulled at the corner of her mouth as if she was remembering something far away. *"He had a son...?"* Suddenly her smile turned into a frown, her scowl deepening more than before. "I must ask you all to leave immediately."

Mona faltered. *Leave it to Jeremy to ruin everything.* "Mrs. Archibald, wait, please!"

She glanced back at Mona, her scowl still in place but her nerves not as poised as before. She was rubbing her arms up and down in small circles, seeming out of sorts. "What is it?" she snapped.

Mona walked forward until she was only steps away from Mrs. Archibald. She took a deep breath and looked up, stealing herself to stay calm. "I'm sorry our visit has upset you, but I promise I'll be a good friend to Pollie. She needs friends, and Jeremy and I want to be those for her." Mona reached into her bag and prayed that what she was about to do would benefit them all.

The tree's words came back to her. *"Bear good fruit. Then passage is granted."* It had said that countless times. Maybe extending grace to this broken woman would count toward that, and help Mona figure out the second half of the tree's riddle.

Mona took her hand out of the bag and revealed a seemingly normal-looking fruit the size of an orange. It was a palish green instead, but aside from that, it looked like it could be a large lime. "I want to give this to you. You don't have to eat it. But I promise you that it's good."

Mona placed the fruit into the unmoving hand of Mrs. Archibald who just stared at it blankly, the shock from their visit finally wearing away at her nerves.

She was quiet and didn't say anything, the crease in her brow losing its fight in staying furrowed. Her silence spoke volumes.

Mona turned to Pollie and lowered her eyes. "I'm so sorry, Pollie. I did everything I could."

Pollie, who had been silent that entire time, stood just as shocked as her mother. Apparently, she too had been surprised by the turn in the conversation.

Mona, her mother, and Jeremy all turned to leave, the silence of what they left behind a heavy weight.

What had Mrs. Archibald been talking about when she mentioned crushed dreams? Had it anything to do with her imagination? What about the tree?

She only had to wonder.

As Real as Fiction

The following morning, Mona sat in Geography, watching and waiting for Pollie to show up. She hadn't been in Algebra earlier, and there was still no sign of her.

Mona couldn't help but feel like it was all her fault. She had ruined their friendship for good.

Jeremy was there though, and he was currently sitting across from her, secretly reading more from his comic book. He'd been reading the same one, *Peter Pan,* for the past month now. Whatever was in there had him extremely captivated.

"Pssst. Jeremy!" Mona whisper-shouted quietly while Mr. Frankweiler began his lecture on tectonic plates and earthquakes.

He looked up from his book and frowned. "What?" he

whisper-shouted back.

"Why do you keep reading that book?"

"I'm not reading so much as I am studying," Jeremy replied, his smirk returning.

"Studying for what?" Mona wanted to whack him off the side of the head sometimes.

"Mona, Jeremy, please. At least pretend to show some interest in what I'm trying to teach the class today," Mr. Frankweiler said from the front of the room, a ruler tapping impatiently in his hand.

"Sorry," they said in unison, trying not to giggle.

Mona turned to face the front of the room but didn't miss Jeremy's last words. "Just wait. I'll tell you at lunch."

Mona sat through the remainder of class counting the seconds. What could Jeremy possibly want to tell her about *Peter Pan?*

By the time the lunch bell rang, Mona felt her pulse quicken. For some reason, she felt like she would be getting answers to some of her questions from the other night. She had put so many hopes on that conversation, but instead, she was left more unsettled than before.

She had so many questions left to be answered. But the first step might be talking to Jeremy. Mona couldn't forget Mrs. Archibald's reaction toward him; it was borderline lunacy. What adult got that worked up over a kid they didn't know?

The two of them filed out of the classroom, along with their classmates, and walked the long hallway to the lunchroom. They found a table in the back corner near a set of windows and sat down. A third person joined them, and when Mona looked up, she saw it was Pollie.

"Pollie!" Mona shouted and ran to hug her friend. "You're here!"

Pollie laughed and hugged Mona back. "I am here! Who would have thought a dentist appointment would take as long as it did?"

"But you're sitting with me...with us! Did your mother...did she...?"

"Yes!" Pollie beamed. "I don't know how you did it, but she relented and said I could be friends with you again. Believe me, I'm just as surprised as you are!"

Mona had never felt this much relief all at once. Here were all three friends together again, at the same table, talking. It was almost too good to be true!

"I never had my doubts," Jeremy said, smiling as he pulled his sandwich out of his bag. He still held fast to his comic book in the other hand. "My guess is the fruit had something to do with it."

"The fruit?" Oh yes! Mona had given Mrs. Archibald one of the strange fruits. But she never expected her to eat it. She half suspected Mrs. Archibald to chuck it in the trash or burn it on the spot.

"Now that you mention it, I did see her eating it this morning. She was in a terrible mood after you left last night, but something altered her before she drove me to the dentist," Pollie mused. "Something about forgiveness and silver dust. I don't know."

Silver dust? Mona glanced at Jeremy's comic book and grew thoughtful. "Why is all of this starting to sound like a fairy tale?" Mona didn't realize she vocalized that last part out loud.

"Because it kind of is…"

And she didn't expect Jeremy to have that kind of answer either.

"Excuse me?" Mona questioned and glanced at Pollie who looked equally as interested, though a little less confused.

"I don't know if you're gonna believe this, but I think aspects of this story are true," Jeremy began, holding up his comic book.

"What aspects?" Mona frowned.

"Well, all of them." Jeremy laughed. "Look, I've been studying what's in this book, and everything lines up. The stories basically read like a history book of my dad's life. He's Peter Pan."

"You've got to be kidding," Mona guffawed, but Pollie had grown quiet. Why wasn't she more shocked? Had Jeremy already talked to her about all of this?

"And your mother is Wendy." Jeremy turned to Pollie, ignoring Mona's incredulity. "What's your mother's maiden name again? Archibald sounds too American."

"Pollie, tell me you think this is ridiculous," Mona interrupted.

"Darling," Pollie answered, smiling as she glanced in Mona's direction. "Her maiden name is Darling!"

What is going on here?

"Precisely. My father changed our last name for professional reasons. Who would take him seriously with a name like Peter Pan?"

"But how can you be certain? Did you see his original birth certificate? What if this is just one big coincidence?" Mona's head was about to fall off.

Jeremy opened his comic to the back page, pulling out a slip of paper before handing it over to Mona. "I snuck a copy of this a few years ago. Open it."

Mona hesitantly complied, unfolding the creases to smooth out the white sheet. She placed it on the table and stared, stunned.

"Please read the lines at the top," Jeremy prompted.

Mona swallowed. "Name of registered child: Peter Pan. Date of birth: August 3, 1911. Place of birth: London, England." She couldn't go on. "Jeremy, this is the birth certificate of someone over 100 years old! There is no way this is your father."

"Ah, but you forget that whilst in Neverland, one never grows up; J.M. Barrie was very clear about that in his first drafts. My dad had to live in Neverland for some years before he came to live permanently in America. That accounts for all those years," Jeremy said it like it was the most obvious solution. "And here is the paper with the name change." Jeremy handed over the document that indicated that the last name Pan had indeed been changed to Panberly.

Mona still had her doubts. "If any of this *is* real, does that mean…are you two? Pollie, your mother is still married, right?" Mona felt like her head was swirling in circles. There was no way Peter Pan was real.

"My parents divorced when I was really young, but I know Jeremy isn't my brother. I've seen pictures of my dad and he's not Jeremy's father," Pollie filled in the gaps. "But I think my mom wishes it was…" A hand flew to her mouth, shock on her face as she looked at Jeremy. "I'm sorry, that's super awkward!"

"No, I figured as much after you told me how often she mutters my dad's name in her sleep." Jeremy laughed. "Besides, I could tell by the way she looked at me last night that I was something of a bad memory to her. I think your mom still loves my dad." Jeremy smirked.

"So, what do you think happened?" Mona questioned, the pieces falling into place. Still, she was having trouble believing their validity.

"My dad left Neverland years ago, returning with Wendy with a promise of marriage. But something must have changed his mind. Otherwise, Pollie would be my sister…"

"And my mother never forgave him…until this morning. She takes any offense personally, hence why she didn't want us being friends," Pollie finished.

"Did he tell you this himself?" Mona looked at Jeremy, eager to learn more.

"Not really, but the signs are everywhere! He's a stevedore at the local docks, feeling more comfortable on the water than he is on land. That accounts for all his years on Hook's ship. I found a thimble in his drawer, and I've occasionally seen his shadow do weird things, like fall in the wrong direction or flinch when he's standing still. He looks like Peter Pan, too. You have to admit that. Here!" Jeremy opened his comic once more and extracted two photos.

What was in that comic book? It was acting more like a scrapbook if anything.

Jeremy placed the two photos on the table, one of J.M. Barrie's illustrated version of Peter and a shot of Jeremy's dad as a kid. It was a striking resemblance. Could all of this be merely a coincidence after all? Mona had to try for one more question; there were still some things unaccounted for.

"But that doesn't explain the seed. What part does that have to play? In any versions I've read of *Peter Pan*, none of them mention one." Mona frowned.

"Ahh, here is where it gets interesting. You know how in the story it says all you need is faith, trust, and pixie dust to fly to the second star to the right? Well, J.M. Barrie only published part of the story. Yes, pixie dust helps you fly and yes, the star is a portal to Neverland, but if you trace the history back far enough, you'll find there's even more to the original story. One of Barrie's earliest drafts had mentioned that the way into Neverland was through a tree. And apparently, pixie dust doesn't just show up out of nowhere, nor is it cultivated by the faeries themselves. It's found in seeds. Silvery, hairy seeds."

Mona's heart sped up. She'd found a seed just like that. The night she'd seen that strange-looking ship in the clouds.

The night she'd wished for a way out of school.

"And these seeds once planted, produce a tree. It's a magical tree and forms a connection with whoever has planted it. It bears all types of fruit in response to the planter's actions and feelings. And above all, the tree serves as a portal to Neverland," Jeremy said confidently. "It's all right here in this book!"

"Your modernized comic book informed you about this age-old legend of *Peter Pan?*" Mona was highly skeptical. There was no way, but still, everything *was* lining up.

"Funny you should ask that…" Jeremy moved to place his comic book in front of Mona and Pollie. From the outside, the cover was indeed a graphic novel, or at least it looked like one, but upon closer examination, Mona could tell there was just a picture glued to the cover and spine. When Jeremy opened up the book itself, Mona was shocked.

"What is this?" Her eyes narrowed in speculation.

Pollie squinted to get a better look, surprise on her face as well.

"I've always known something was weird with my family, so I've been researching over the years. Every story and version of *Peter Pan* I come across, I cut it out and glue it in here, pictures included. This isn't actually a graphic novel, it's just a notebook disguised to look like one." Jeremy smirked again. "So, it's kind of like an endless cycle of the story on repeat, each version providing more and more of a history. I've even traced back Barrie's earlier unpublished versions in this bad boy." Jeremy patted his little book with pride. "That's how I found out about the seeds and the magical fruit."

Mona felt like she could believe him a little better now, but how did she know this story pertained to her friends' lives?

"But how is this possible? Are you sure this story relates to your parents?" Mona ran her hands through her hair, tangling them in the process.

"Yes, I think Jeremy's right, Mone. Our mom and dad are *the* Peter and *the* Wendy from the story. Jeremy isn't the only one with the evidence. My mother has sketchbooks hidden in her nightstand, and on some occasions when she's out, I'll go in and look at them. The pictures are bizarre—mermaids, crocodiles, and boys dressed in animal costumes and leaves. She's drawn herself beside them as if reminiscing on times when she was Wendy from the stories. Not to mention I've even found the name '*Wendy Pan*' written on rolled-up pieces of paper in the trash can. I find it an odd hobby for someone who has practically raised me to ward off imagination like the plague. The evidence is everywhere. And your tree is *our* portal to Neverland."

"Our portal? Guys, I've been taking care of that tree for a month, and not once has it ever shown me a portal to anywhere!" *If so, I wouldn't have gone to school in the first place.*

This whole *Peter Pan* business was getting out of hand. Mona was even beginning to feel bad for Mrs. Archibald because of it. But the puzzle *was* coming together. Why couldn't it be true?

Mona remembered the day when the magic tree first spoke to her, and her hands in her hair stilled instantly. "*Bear good fruit. Then passage is granted.*" It had said those words countless times; did passage mean a portal to Neverland? Could it actually be true?

"I don't think it's ready yet. There needs to be a sign." Jeremy closed his book.

What kind of sign? Had Mona missed it all those weeks of taking care of the tree? But instead of asking those questions, a different one came to mind.

"Why do you want to go to Neverland so badly?" Mona asked him.

"I," he paused briefly as if he was choosing his words carefully. "I guess I want to get more answers to this whole story." He shrugged, like that was the obvious answer.

But Mona could tell there was more to what he was saying. What was he not telling them?

The table grew quiet, the weight of everything settling down like dust. This had been a very interesting lunch. None of them had touched their meals. And at this rate, Mona felt like she wouldn't be able to stomach food for a few days. There was enough information to digest on its own.

Chapter 21

Neverland

Mona made her bed and tugged on some clean clothes. She looked at her alarm clock and sighed in relief; it read 10:00 AM—still plenty of time. Her parents had told her to be downstairs by 10:05 at the latest.

Today was finally Saturday, the day she was to turn thirteen! She didn't want a party, but she did ask her parents if Pollie and Jeremy could come over at some point.

She'd shower tomorrow morning; today, she wanted to soak in the sun and get outside as fast as she could.

On her way down the stairs, she heard noises coming from the kitchen. Mona rounded the corner to find her parents and Lisa, a cake freshly lit, waiting for her.

"She's awake!" Lisa shouted!

All three of them quickly began singing "Happy Birthday" before the candles threatened to melt the frosting.

Mona watched contentedly, her smile wide.

They finished and everyone clapped enthusiastically.

"Happy birthday, sweetheart!" her mother said, hugging her tight.

"Yes, happy birthday, my girl." Her father hugged her too.

"Happy birthday to the best sister around!" Lisa joined them and squeezed everyone even tighter,

Their love warmed Mona's heart. She hadn't been expecting this.

The sound of the doorbell ringing interrupted their hug; her father looked over his shoulder at the clock on the stove. "Ah, perfect timing! Just in time to eat some cake!" He chuckled, winking at Mona.

"We wanted to do something special for you before your friends got here." Her mother smiled.

"They're here already?" Mona pulled out of their embrace and ran to the front door, yanking it open wide to find Pollie, Jeremy, and Ariel standing there with cheeky grins on their faces.

"Happy birthday!" they shouted in unison. In each of their hands was a present.

"Thank you for coming!" Mona hugged them all and

brought them inside.

Once in the house, Mona introduced Jeremy and Pollie to her father and sister before they all dug into the cake; it was a delicious chocolate with buttercream frosting. The perfect breakfast food.

By the time everyone finished and put their plates in the sink, it was nearing 11:00.

"Mona, why don't you go spend some time outside with your friends! We'll clean up in here. The morning won't last forever." Her motioned them toward the door as she began to clean the dishes.

"Thanks, Mom! Thanks, everyone!" She hugged her parents and turned to leave with her friends before stopping. Something didn't feel right; she looked over at her sister who appeared disappointed. "Leese, Ariel, want to come with us?"

Lisa and Ariel's eyes grew wide and they nodded eagerly, clearly taken by surprise.

The five of them exited the house and went into the backyard. It was a beautiful morning; the air was chilly and the sun was shining even though the sky was filled with clouds.

Speaking of clouds, as Mona looked up at the sky, her breath hitched in her throat. There it was again! *The ship.* A graceful cloud flitted across the sky, sailing in and out of the sun, its silver sheen leaving a stream of silver in its wake. *It must be real. It has to be.*

"Do you guys see that?" Mona pointed in the direction of the ship, excitement in her words.

"It's the sign!" Jeremy shouted. "It's gotta be!"

"Mona, where's the tree?" Pollie tugged on Mona's hand.

"What sign? What are you guys talking about?" Lisa questioned.

"I don't see the ship!" Ariel cried.

"Quick, follow me!" Mona led everyone to the hidden alcove, their steps following close behind hers.

She stepped through the surrounding trees and entered the small enclosure, her friends right beside her. Her voice caught in her throat. This was not the grove she had remembered.

"It's-it's all giant!" Mona scanned the small enclosure in bewilderment and marveled at the faerie houses which were now perched high in the sky as if growing into trees themselves. They towered around the magic tree whose timber loomed before her. It had grown astronomically since the last time she'd seen it, and it was completely silver from top to bottom. On its boughs hung the same pale pink stars, the ones she had tasted a few weeks ago; some also had fallen and were scattered along the ground. And at the very top of the tree hovered the ship shrouded in cloud.

There it is again! The hair on Mona's neck stood on end and her stomach dipped in somersaults. This sight before her was like nothing she had ever seen!

"It's the portal!" Pollie breathed in awe.

"The portal to where?" Lisa grabbed Mona's hand, fear suddenly seeming to take hold of her.

"To Neverland!" Jeremy said, his eyes wide with wonder. "Come on, let's go!"

"Jeremy, I'm scared!" Ariel hesitated.

Jeremy took his sister's hand and assured her all would be well. That seemed to mollify her as she walked with him toward the glistening bark.

Mona looked at Pollie and nodded. They stepped forward, ready to touch the trunk too.

This is what Mona had wanted all along, what she had wished and prayed for since the start of school. But she was glad it hadn't happened then.

Over the course of a month, she had learned it was better to face her fears rather than run away from them. There was strength in telling the truth, and there was also strength in numbers. She had made friends even when she thought she wouldn't, and what better way to venture to Neverland than to go with the children of Peter and Wendy themselves.

Mona paused and saw Lisa standing timidly by the

entrance of the alcove. She hadn't budged since they'd first arrived.

"Lisa, are you coming or not?" Mona held out her hand.

"I-I don't know. Is it safe?" Lisa hesitated, seeing how tightly Ariel clasped onto her brother's arm.

"I can't guarantee it's safe, but you'll have us. We'll look after you. It's only for a short visit," Mona assured her.

"But what are you hoping to find there?" Lisa asked as she stepped closer, her hand now in Mona's. She looked doubtful like she wanted to ask a million questions.

At that moment, all five of them placed their hands on the trunk of the tree. Mona's palm tingled, a wave of wind encircling them all in a gentle cyclone.

A sweet aroma wafted in the air, reminding Mona that the change in the tree had largely been because of her *bearing good fruit*. The portal only opened because she had learned what it meant to be honest with herself and others. She still had a lot of learning do, but she could confidently say that the fruit she was bearing was indeed good. It was some of the best she'd ever tasted.

"What are you hoping to find there?" Lisa repeated her question, yelling so her voice could be heard above the wind.

All of a sudden, the tree began to shake and the wind howled even louder.

"My mother, of course," Jeremy said as he held fast to his sister, his dimpled smile the last thing Mona saw before a silver spark exploded and the five of them vanished.

Silver raindrops fell from the sky as the clouded ship winked and disappeared along with them. All that was left was a spattering of silver dust wafting in the wind.

The End.

Acknowledgements

I would be remiss if I didn't thank the host of people who helped make this novel possible. The more I continue to write, the more I realize just how important a community of cheerleaders, critiquers (yes, I'm convinced that's a real word), and friends are.

For my family, thank you for believing in me and bearing with me as I spent even more hours writing and talking about writing this past year.

For the sweet girls at my church for who I originally began this story, thank you for reading it and loving it at its weakest, and for giving me the motivation and encouragement to keep going.

For my incredible beta readers: Kailey Jessop, Anna Augustine, Anna Deaton, Anna Wolfe, Rachael Crisanti, and Tara Staniszewski. I am indebted to you all, and I am very grateful, not only for your willingness to help but for your friendships.

And a huge and special thank you to my dear friend and editor, Jordan Yaworski, who read all four drafts and provided quality feedback each go around. This novel wouldn't be nearly as good without all your help. You are simply the best!

For my cover designer, Germancreative, I am blown away by your design—you have made the story come to life.

For my wonderful internal format editor, Michelle M. Bruhn. Thank you for making my book look pristine and beautifully cohesive on the inside.

For my cat, Moo. You had absolutely nothing to do with this novel, but nonetheless, you were ever-present. Thanks for being such a good boy like always.

For my beloved husband, Zac. Thank you for being my rock and confidant. You help me more than you know. Love you always.

For my Lord and Savior, Jesus Christ. Thank you for giving me inspiration and the ability to put these words on paper. I pray I did them justice.

And lastly, thank YOU, my readers, for picking up this book and believing in me. You make this writing journey as sweet as a good piece of fruit.